Also by Sydney Canyon

Novellas:

Bella Vita

Fine

Igniting Temptation

Miracle at Christmas

One Night

Shadow's Eyes

Light Reading: A Collection of Novellas

Acknowledgements

Special thanks to my amazing and wonderful editor, Caralee. You strengthened my writing and pushed me to make this an even better story.

Second Chance

By

Sydney Canyon

2015

Second Chance © 2015 Sydney Canyon
Triplicity Publishing, LLC

ISBN-13: 978-0996242929
ISBN-10: 0996242929

This is a work of fiction. Names, characters, places, and incidents are the product of the author's imagination and are used fictitiously. Any resemblance to actual persons, living or dead, business establishments, events of any kind, or locales is entirely coincidental.

Printed in the United States of America
First Edition – 2015

Cover Design: Triplicity Publishing, LLC
Interior Design: Triplicity Publishing, LLC
Editor: Caralee Anley - Triplicity Publishing, LLC

Dedication

This book is for all of those who have fought the war on terror, become disabled, suffer from PTSD, and lost their lives.

To my wife: Without you, I wouldn't be where I am today.

Prologue

The incoming insurgent fire bombarded the left side of the eight-wheeled light armored vehicle, sending shrapnel and sparks flying through the pitch-black of the desert night sky. The popping noise of the rounds hitting the metal exterior was excruciatingly loud. Flashes of light echoed in all directions, lighting up the night. The six Marines inside the Bravo One LAV-25 watched the scene unfold before them on the viewing screen as their convoy continued their reconnaissance mission. Dust clouds rolled around them on makeshift roads as their speed increased. The two-way radio crackled back and forth, mixing with the pinging of the bullets flying overhead.

"Left flank up ahead, Bravo One!" a male voice yelled across the radio.

"No," said the Staff Sergeant sitting in the command seat of Bravo One, mostly to herself as she used a pen light to study the map in her hand, comparing it to the terrain on the radar screen in front of her.

"What was that, Staff Sergeant?" asked Corporal Davidson as he fought to steer the bouncing vehicle.

"I said no, Davidson. They are going the wrong the way!" she yelled, switching the channel on her two-way radio to communicate with the lead vehicle of the convoy. "Alpha One, you missed the mark. We need to go another two miles before we turn. The checkpoint is further west," she barked into the radio. "We need to go around this insurgent group, not through it!" she yelled.

It was unclear whether the Second Lieutenant in the lead LAV heard her message or not, but the vehicle turned at the next path on the left, leading the convoy directly into the heart of the enemy fire that had been hovering around them.

"Damn it!" she yelled.

"What do I do?" the Corporal asked.

"Never break up the convoy. Go, go, go!" she shouted and turned to the gunner, along with the three scout troops in the back of the vehicle. Lance Corporal Wilkerson, Corporal Smith, and Corporal Leonard were firing machine guns through the tiny slit openings in the window panels. Corporal Mulky was in the middle seat, in control of the .25mm chain gun on the turret mounted to the top of the vehicle.

"How are we on ammo?" she asked.

"Plenty of shells," Corporal Mulky answered.

She said a silent prayer to make it out of this hellhole to their next checkpoint.

Less than a minute later, she heard the distinctive screeching of the rocket-propelled grenade rounds before she saw the thin line of the orange tail flame on the screen. The insurgents had obviously launched the RPGs from somewhere out in the distance and by the time she found the incoming grenades it was too late. There wasn't time to brace for the impact, much less try to avoid them. The force of the three explosions shattered the armored plating up front where the driver was sitting. Bits of shrapnel sprayed in all directions.

The front of the left side of the LAV had literally exploded when the first grenade slammed into it. Then, the second grenade rocked the vehicle violently as it slammed the left side, just before the final impact, which caved in the left rear like a tin can. The front section immediately caught fire from the explosion and flames began licking their way back towards the turret.

It was silent for a split second before the sound of more rounds pinging against the metal rang in the Staff Sergeant's ears, bringing her back to focus. She couldn't see anything but darkness. Her eyes burned like her face was on fire. She screamed in pain as she tried to move around in the tight, mangled compartment. She could barely get half of a breath into her lungs. Her chest felt like it had been crushed. The air around her was full of smoke and dust. Warm red blood spewed from her mouth rolling down her chin as she coughed and gagged. She heard sounds coming from somewhere inside the vehicle. Thankfully, someone else was alive. As least she thought she was still alive. "Davidson, can you hear me?" she rasped. There was no answer. "Wilkerson, Leonard, Smith, Mulky, can any of you hear me?" she tried again. She silently prayed that the lead vehicle had made it past the insurgent attack and that the rest of the convoy had turned back, but at the same time, she hoped they checked for survivors.

"Come on guys, we have to get out of here," she held her breath as she moved towards the seat in front of her where the driver had been sitting. She ran her hands across his chest through the sticky and warm substance covering his flak jacket. Reaching for his head, she stuck her hands into something warm and squishy like raw meat, which was also covered with the same thick wet substance...*blood...no! NO!*

She realized her hands were feeling what was left of his face. Her body recoiled and her eyes opened. Everything was still pitch black. She screamed in agony from the searing pain she felt in that split second then quickly squished her eyes closed once again, reverting back to feeling her way around in the total darkness. Her eyes were burning badly, so she squeezed them shut as hard as she could. She coughed and choked as more blood poured from her mouth. She finally grabbed something towards the turret seat that felt human. *An arm...*She pulled as hard as she could, screaming in pain as her chest constricted.

She finally pulled the body over the seat as she felt for a pulse. *He's alive. Oh, thank God.* She felt the heat from the fire and knew the flames were dangerously close to where she had been sitting. The left section of the LAV roof was peeled back like a tin can. She pulled the young man against her. Slowly, using her legs, she slid out of the vehicle on her back with him on top of her. She could hear gunfire in the distance. The distinct sound of the AK-47 rifles made her cringe. The enemy was obviously getting closer.

"Don't leave me, Sarge," he whispered.

"I'll be right back." She laid him on his back and crawled back into the vehicle.

By this time she was coughing frantically and spitting puddles of blood. Her lungs burned and her chest throbbed with every short intake of breath. Her face was wet from either tears or blood running down her cheeks from her stinging eyes. She felt her way around once again, touching everything until she came in contact with something human near the rear cargo area. She could hear the stray bullets from the enemy gunfire hitting the side of the wreckage.

"Can you hear me?" She coughed and spewed more blood as she spoke. She could feel the warm sticky liquid running down her chin to her neck. The vehicle was full of smoke, causing her to cough twice as much as she struggled to breathe. She fumbled around the body searching for a pulse until she reached his head and realized his neck was broken and he wasn't breathing. "No!" she yelled.

Something grabbed her arm and pulled her.

"Help me," the voice whispered.

She touched the hand pulling on her and felt her way up until she could grip his flak jacket. Then, she reached up to touch his face. Realizing he was alive, she pulled him back against her chest. Every shallow breath that she took felt like it may be her last. She knew something was seriously wrong with her eyes and her chest, but she pushed hard as she maneuvered herself through the mangled wreckage, pulling the man along with her towards the twisted shards of burnt steel and singed wires hanging down overhead. Searing hot flames had reached the crumpled hole of the emergency hatch that she was using to crawl through the vehicle. Thick black smoke filled her lungs as the flames scorched the edges of her uniform. She held her breath and pulled as hard as she could until she and the man in her arms were out of the wreckage.

She laid him next to the other Marine and turned away when her stomach retched. She coughed a couple of times as she felt the thick, warm liquid come up the back of her throat. As she puked, she was sure the rancid, bitter taste of saltwater and rusted metal in her mouth was blood.

"Staff Sergeant?" rasped the young man who was leaning with her against the opposite side of the burning wreckage. She wiped her mouth on her sleeve and turned back to him.

"What?" she said as she coughed again.

"Enemy fire—"

"I know. They're on the other side," she stopped to cough and spit more of the warm, sticky blood from her mouth. "We're okay for now."

Chapter 1

One week later, Darien woke up in Walter Reed Medical Center in Washington, D.C. The first thing she noticed was everything was dark, very dark. Her chest hurt. Her throat burned. Her head felt like it was about to explode.

"Hello?" she whispered hoarsely as she ran her hands up and down her arms, feeling the IV lines protruding from her body. *Why can't I see anything?* "Hello, is anyone there?" She tried a little louder.

"Ssshh. Your throat is still tender."

"I can't see. Where am I?"

"You're in the hospital. I'm Dr. Nelson. Do you know your name?" the doctor asked as he checked her vitals.

"I'm United States Marine Corps Staff Sergeant, Darien Hollister."

"Good."

"I can't see. What's wrong with my eyes?" She tried again and everything was still completely black. She couldn't tell whether her eyes were open or closed.

"Your eyes were hurt in the accident, Staff Sergeant Hollister."

"Am I blind?" she whispered.

He sighed and squeezed her hand. "I'm afraid so. Shrapnel sliced through your corneas down to the anterior chambers of your retinas. There was nothing we could do. I'm sorry."

Tears silently rolled down her cheeks. When Dr. Nelson moved to let go of her hand, she squeezed. "What about the other soldiers in my convoy?"

"Lance Corporal Michael Wilkerson had two broken ribs, a concussion, and minor cuts and bruises. Corporal Harlowe Mulky also had a concussion plus a dislocated shoulder and bruised hip. They have both been released. I was told you saved both of their lives."

"I...all I did was pull them from the LAV," she said quietly.

"Yes...but, Staff Sergeant, you not only pulled two grown men from a burning, mangled wreck, you did it blind with a collapsed and punctured lung, as well as four broken ribs." He squeezed her hand again.

"I remember the other three Marines?" She paused, "Davidson, Smith, and Leonard—"

"Yes ma'am, they all died from the impact of the RPGs. There was nothing you could have done for any of them," he sighed and stepped back from the bed.

Over the past six years, since the beginning of the war, Dr. Nelson had seen a number of various injuries come through the Army Hospital. This one seemed to hit him the hardest.

When he left the room, Darien reached up to touch her eyes, letting the tears flow freely. She sobbed until there was nothing left inside of her.

Chapter 2

Darien hadn't been home in over a year after being deployed to Afghanistan. Now, she was sitting on the beach in Oceanside, California, the only place she ever really called home, staring out at the sunset that looked like complete darkness to her. It had been three months since the attack on her convoy and the damage to her eyes was tremendous, preventing her from using the subtle differences in black and gray shadows that most sight-impaired people relied on. She let the sand run through her hands, trying to remember what it looked like.

When she had been released from the hospital, she'd gone to a rehabilitation center for another three weeks to learn how to live as a blind person. After that, the Marine Corps decorated her with various medals and achievements for her service and gave her an honorable medical discharge. At that very moment, the tiny part of her life that had still existed shattered to pieces. She'd just turned thirty-four years old. Her career had been ripped out from under her, and it had taken everything she knew right along with it.

She reached down and filled her palm with sand once more, letting it slide through her fingers. She had stopped crying long ago. She didn't hate the world. In fact, she was sure she completely skipped over being mad and went straight to depression. She couldn't live alone for at least a year according to her doctor, and she was tired of depending on someone to be there for her twenty-four hours a day, seven days a week. She thought about putting her condo up for sale since it was on the sixth floor, and she still couldn't figure out how to read Braille. She constantly bumped into things in her home, and her gourmet cooking days were also over. She purchased a microwave with Braille writing under the numbers and words, so that she could at least attempt to make some foods. Yet she still struggled with learning the sequence of raised dots.

Her mind drifted as she felt the coolness of the night start to work its way across her bare arms. She continued to run the sand through her fingers, listening to the waves crash against the shore. She tried desperately to remember what the waves looked like. She could barely remember what she looked like anymore. She was stuck in a world of complete darkness.

The voice next to her brought her attention back to reality.

"What would you like for dinner?" Val asked.

Darien wanted to say nothing, but she knew she had to eat. Her cousin, Valerie, had been a huge help since she found out about the accident and flew to Washington, D.C. with Darien's parents. Val and Darien had been best friends since Val was six and Darien was eight when Darien beat up a boy that was picking on Val in elementary school. When Darien was released from the hospital, Val insisted on moving in to take care of her and had been her rock for the past three months. Darien's parents were thankful for Val's assistance since they lived in Arizona and still worked full-time jobs. They wouldn't have been able to take care of their daughter unless she'd moved back to her childhood home, which she'd refused to do.

Darien had moved to Oceanside when the Marine Corps stationed her at Camp Pendleton eight years earlier and Val was living 45 minutes away in San Diego, so they saw each other often and had remained best friends over the years.

"How about pizza?" Darien suggested.

She wasn't ready to sit in a restaurant. The only time she ever left the house was to take the ten-minute drive down to the beach. Since the day she was released from the hospital, she'd worn a dark pair of Oakley sunglasses to cover her eyes, but she'd started taking them off in the house two weeks ago. This new act had made Val believe her cousin was finally starting the slow turn towards some kind of normalcy. The doctors had told her before she brought Darien home that it could be six months before the wounded woman would allow other people to see her blindness. The doctors had also given her a bunch of pamphlets on Post Traumatic Stress Disorder to help with Darien's adjustment.

Val turned towards her and smiled. Even though the sun had set and it was dark outside, Darien was still wearing her dark glasses. She was getting better at telling time since she was learning how to read the changes in the temperature throughout the day.

"Pizza? Dare, you have to eat more than pizza, babe. How about I cook us some grilled chicken and vegetables?" Val said.

Darien smiled at the childhood nickname her cousin had always called her as she stood, brushed the sand off her pants and turned towards Val. She sighed, "Chicken it is."

Val jumped up and smiled, then grabbed her hand to lead her out of the sand towards the car. "You need a haircut," she murmured.

"Really? I hadn't noticed," Darien replied, pulling her walking stick from her pocket and snapping it open with a flick of her wrist. She hated using it, but if she ever wanted to learn to live alone again, she'd need to get used to using the stick to help her find her way and keep her safe. The doctor had also suggested getting a seeing-eye dog, but she wasn't ready for that step. Val thought otherwise and had made an appointment for the next day at the rehab center that handled the dogs.

***

"I don't need a dog, Val." Darien said as they walked into the doctor's office for Darien's check up. She was supposed to follow up with the Ophthalmologist every month for six months so that he could keep up with the changes in her optical nerves.

"Darien, you will eventually. Why not start now? You and the dog could learn together." Val tried again as she signed her cousin in at the desk.

"I can barely take care of myself right now, Val. How the hell am I supposed to take care of a dog?" She raised her voice a little louder than she meant to.

Val blew out a frustrated breath and led her to an empty pair of chairs. "Those dogs are trained—" She was cut off when a woman came out of the side door.

"Staff Sergeant Hollister, the doctor will see you now."

"Already?" Darien's face scrunched. They'd had to wait a half hour at her last appointment.

"Yes ma'am. As a matter of fact, he's been expecting you," the assistant said as she led them to the exam room. When she walked away, Val turned to Darien. She had taken her glasses off once she heard the door handle click, but her eyes were closed.

"What's that all about?" Val murmured, wondering why the doctor was so anxious to see them.

"I don't know. Maybe he's bored." Darien shrugged and ran her hand through her short, spiky brown hair as the door opened once again.

"Good morning, ladies." Dr. Feldman stepped into the room holding Darien's chart and pulled the rolling stool over to her. "I hear you're thinking of getting a dog."

"No, I'm not," Darien growled through clenched teeth. The doctor laughed when he saw Val shaking her head yes.

"So, why don't you want a dog, Staff Sergeant?"

She wasn't ready to talk about her personal life to this man and she was tired of everyone calling her by her rank. She was no longer part of this country's military. She was a retired veteran, something she never thought she'd be until she was at least fifty. Although, she still sat ramrod straight and presented herself as someone with a high-ranking military caliber. She could get out of the Marines, but she couldn't get the Marines out of her. "I'm allergic to dogs, Dr. Feldman," she answered simply.

"Oh, well there are allergy pills that can help with that. But, a dog isn't the reason for your visit today," he added, setting her chart on the table next to her as he slid closer.

He took his pen light in one hand and opened each of her eyelids, flashing the light in them one at a time. Her eyes were solid white and slightly milky grey where the pupils and irises had been. They were severely damaged in the accident and had been removed during surgery. Val turned her head. Even though she had seen them before, it still hurt her to see what her cousin and best friend was going through.

When the doctor finished the notes in Darien's chart, he turned back towards her. "How do you feel about experimental procedures?"

Darien cocked her head to the side. "What exactly do you mean by that?"

He cleared his throat and gripped her hand. "A colleague of mine brought something to my attention a week ago, and I immediately thought of you. A doctor named Harry Norton has performed a small number of moderately successful and highly experimental eye transplants." He heard Darien and Val gasp at the same time. "Keep in mind this is an organ transplant and many times there are complications. Dr. Norton, as I said, has been somewhat successful. I believe you may be a candidate for this procedure. That is, of course, if this is something you would consider."

"Uh—" Darien was speechless.

"What are the complications? How many has he done?" Val was spitting questions off the top of her head. Dr. Feldman held his hand up to stall her interrogation.

"I contacted Dr. Norton last week and asked him to send me some information for you and your family to take a look at." He handed Val a couple of pamphlets. "There are complications with any organ transplant, particularly with infections that cause the body to reject

14

the new organs. Currently, there are a vast number of immune system medications that help reduce the threat of infections. Also, there is a very high risk of the procedure failing, which means you will still not be able to see even with the new eyes." He paused.

"Now, as far as the ratio of success, Dr. Norton has performed exactly three of these transplants. So far only one of them has been successful. This person has fully restored vision in both eyes. One of the three had a stroke and passed away during the operation. The remaining recipient has had mixed results. His body rejected the new eyes at first, but slowly the nerves are starting to grow together. Some days he can see a little and most days he is still blind."

He squeezed Darien's hand. "Staff Sergeant Hollister, the choice is yours. There is a small chance that this doctor can give you your sight back. But, there is a bigger chance that you may have complications during or after the transplant surgery. Plus, you will have to rely on daily medication for the rest of your life to keep your body from rejecting the organs."

Darien felt weightless. She wasn't sure she was even breathing. The room felt as if it was closing in on her rapidly with every heartbeat and shallow breath. She'd never hyperventilated or fainted in her life, but she was sure it was about to happen if she didn't get outside soon. "I need some time to digest this, Dr. Feldman. I...I think I may be in shock." She felt his large warm hand squeeze hers again.

"Sure, I don't expect you to make a decision this serious without thinking it through. You have my number." He paused to look at Val. "Call me if you have any questions. There is a process to follow, so this is not something that will happen overnight."

"Thank you, doctor. I appreciate everything you have done for me over these past few months," Darien said as she stood and waited for Val to lead her out of the office. She stopped to take a deep breath when she hit the warm air and felt the sunshine on her face.

"Want to go to the beach?" Val asked. She knew that was the only place Darien allowed herself to relax. Val didn't try to understand what Darien had been going through. All she knew was the numerous nightmares she'd witnessed where Darien awoke with tears of anger and sadness.

Chapter 3

Darien sat in front of the waves with the scorching sun beating down on her face and the coarse grains of tan, Southern California sand, slipping through her fingers like an hourglass. It had been three months since Dr. Feldman had told her about Dr. Norton and his success stories. She'd met with him right away and begun taking the immune system boosters to prepare her body for the transplant surgery. She was the next recipient on the waiting list for the experimental surgery. To say that she was nervous would be an understatement. She wanted desperately to see again, but that actually scared her more than the surgery process of having her own eyes removed and someone else's eyes attached in their place. It frightened her because if she could see, then she'd have to face the reality of her new life. Since the attack, everything was covered in darkness—the various pictures on her walls from her tours, the uniforms hanging in her closet—the life she used to lead. The waiting game was an emotional rollercoaster. Any time, any day, she could receive the call that she was waiting for; the call saying they had a donor. It could be in ten minutes or two years. She tried to remember what life was like before the accident. That seemed like another lifetime; a time when she was happy, enjoyed her job, and took her sight for granted. In one split second, her world was ripped out from under her. Tears ran down her cheeks when she tried to picture a sunset and couldn't. She was stuck in a life of total darkness. She cried a little harder as she thought about the only way for a pair of donor eyes to come available. Someone would have to die. She hated knowing that she'd be benefiting from someone's death.

Darien looked up at the sky and let the heat from the sun dry her tear-stained face. She had never been a very emotional person, not until the day she woke up in the dark. It took her a full month before she was ready to stand up on a stage in her full dress uniform, in front of her parents, Val, and a select group of her peers. She received the commending Silver Star and Purple Heart medals from the President of the United States for her meritorious service and sacrifice in the War on Terrorism. She knew there were reporters and TV cameras close to the stage. She could hear the commotion. It wasn't until later that Val told her she'd been on national television. She wasn't exactly pleased that the ceremony had been televised, but she'd understood why.

That same day Darien had also signed her Honorable Discharge papers. She could no longer serve her country and do the only job she had ever known because she was blind. She still wasn't able to adjust to being out of the military. The fact that she couldn't see meant her life had already changed drastically. Since she was eighteen years old, the only life she'd known was the United States Marine Corps. It felt weird being a civilian. Fortunately no one had come up to her saying they'd recognized her from the news stories about the attack on her convoy or receiving medals from the President. But she was going to be the center of a media circus once again when a donor became available. That thought didn't appeal to her at all.

Darien had barely spoken about the procedure or the fact that she was probably going to be able to see again. Maybe not perfectly, and maybe not even in both eyes, but at least she would see something besides total darkness. Every time Val or her parents mentioned anything about her eyes, she simply changed the subject or left the room.

"Sun's setting soon."

"I know. I can feel it." Darien didn't have to turn around. She knew her cousin's voice and had heard her walk up nearly five minutes earlier.

Since losing her sight, her hearing had taken on a dramatic change in sensitivity. She felt like she had dog ears. She barely slept most nights because she heard every single sound in the house. It drove her nuts.

***

Darien had just sat down at the dinner table when Val's cell phone rang loudly. She listened as Val answered and told whomever it was to hold on.

"It's for you," Val said, grabbing her hand to place the phone in it.

"If it's my parents, tell them I'll call them later." Darien pulled her hand away.

"It's Dr. Norton," Val whispered.

Darien turned her head towards Val's voice and reached her hand out. "Hello?" she answered, holding the phone to her ear.

"Darien, it's time," he said. "You have a donor and the organs are on a private jet, headed this way as we speak."

"Okay," she murmured in shock. Pulling the phone from her ear, she whispered, "There's a donor."

Val immediately grabbed the phone to get all of the details from the doctor. She ran to the kitchen to write down the specifics. Darien was sitting at the dining table with her head in her hands as she took in one labored breath after the other, letting them out slowly.

"Are you sure you want to do this?" Val asked, patting her shoulder.

"There's nothing I want more than to see again."

"What if it doesn't work, Darien? Is it worth going through another surgery?"

"I thought we went over all of this?" Darien huffed.

"We did. I'm just making sure."

"Val, it's a done deal. I know the consequences. It's my life. This is what I want." She pushed her chair back from the table and reached for her walking cane. "What's our timeline?"

Val smiled at the woman in front of her. The rigid composure and stern temperament of a military officer were drilled so deeply into Darien. A lifetime could go by and she would still be a Marine.

"We have to check in at the hospital in half an hour," Val answered.

"What are we waiting for then?"

In all honestly, they weren't waiting for anything. Darien had insisted that they have a bag packed and ready to go in case they got the call and needed to rush out. The only thing Val needed to do was get her in the car and to the hospital.

"You need to call your parents," Val said while she watched Darien walk down the hall towards her room with the walking stick bouncing off the baseboards as she found her way.

"You can call them when the surgery starts," Darien said as she changed into a pair of black gym shorts and a dark gray t-shirt with USMC written across the front in black letters. She pulled on a black pair of running socks and her sneakers before walking back into the living room. "I'm ready," she called out, turning her head when she heard footsteps on the right.

"Your parents will be on the next plane," Val informed, grabbing her hand.

"You called them already?"

"Of course, damn it. You can't do this alone."

"I'm not alone. You're here. Now come on before I figure out how to drive us there myself."

Val shook her head and helped Darien to the car before going back in for the packed bag.

***

The surgery had taken four long hours. Dr. Norton walked into the waiting room with his mask pulled down off his face. Val jumped from her seat next to Darien's parents.

"Her optic nerves gave us a bit of hassle, but everything went smoothly," he said.

"Can she see?" Darien's mother asked.

"These are Darien's parents, Paula and Mike Hollister," Val added.

"I'm pleased to meet you both." Dr. Norton smiled softly, then sighed, "I'm afraid we won't know anything for at least twenty-four hours. She's in recovery now, but we have her heavily sedated. We don't want her to stress out the new organs."

"We understand," Paula said.

"Can we see her?" Val asked.

"I'll have the nurse come get you once she's been moved from recovery."

Mr. Hollister stood up, hugging his wife and niece as they cried tears of hope. Darien had already been through so much in the last seven months. They weren't sure how she'd handle it if the surgery failed.

***

Darien's father had spent the rest of the night on the couch in the intensive care waiting room, while Paula and Val curled up in chairs in Darien's room. The nurses had checked on her continuously throughout the night and into the next day. The doctor had called that morning and instructed the staff to slowly reduce the medication that was keeping her sedated.

Dr. Norton finally arrived later that afternoon and asked the family to wait down the hall while he removed the bandages and checked her eyes.

"Darien, can you hear me?" he asked, squeezing her hand as he watched her begin to wake up. "Come on, I know you're fuzzy, but I need you to wake up for me."

The nurse held a cup of water close to her with a straw at Darien's lips. She took a few small sips and cleared her throat.

"I'm sorry. The medication we gave you makes everyone feel like they've been steamrolled and eaten a bag of cotton balls," Dr. Norton laughed.

Darien cleared her throat a few times. "Did it work?" she rasped.

"We're about to find out." He instructed the nurse to turn the lights completely out as he began removing the bandages. "What do you see?" he asked.

"Darkness," Darien murmured.

"That's to be expected. It's dark in here." He shined his penlight on the wall above her.

"I see light!" she exclaimed.

"Good. I don't want to stress the eyes, so we're going to cover them back up for a couple more days. I'm going to keep you in here a little longer so we can keep a close watch on you and make sure your new eyes get the drops they need every two hours."

"Do you think I can see since I saw the light?" she asked as he put new bandages on her eyes.

"Well, you couldn't tell light from dark before the surgery, so that's a good sign. We'll talk more in a few days. Take it easy. Stress builds pressure in the eyes and blood vessels, and we definitely don't want that."

***

When the doctor returned a few days later, the bandages over Darien's eyes were removed, and she saw shadows in the dark room. He worked the light up to a medium level slowly over the next couple of days. Darien's eyes focused a little more as the light was increased in the room, until she was able to fully recognize everything in the dim lighting.

She'd become a little nearsighted with her new eyes so Dr. Norton had ordered her a pair of glasses to wear outside at night. She was instructed to only wear dark sunglasses that completely covered her eyes while outside during the day, so he ordered her prescription sunglasses as well.

The only issue she seemed to have was the loss of her peripheral version. She could see straight ahead and up and down nearly thirty feet before it started to become a little blurry, but there was also this black wall, built up on both sides of her face, extending out nearly six inches. Dr. Norton told her that would probably never go away, but it didn't matter as long as she could see again.

Chapter 4

Six months after the surgery, Darien was fully recovered and had finally gotten used to the loss of her peripheral vision. She hated wearing the prescription glasses at night and went without them on most occasions. She'd been a ball of mixed emotions since the day she'd opened her eyes and saw her family's faces. Knowing someone had to die for her to be able to see again had broken her heart. Enough death and destruction followed her as it was—this only added to the pile that weighed heavily on her shoulders. She still hadn't gotten used to seeing the bright, turquoise blue eyes staring back at her in the mirror. Hers had been a dull shade of brown, and the change made her feel like she was looking at a stranger.

Darien had sat on the beach for weeks, silently thanking her donor as she watched the sun rise and set, until she'd finally decided the only way she could move on with her newfound sight was to find the donor's family and thank them for the gift she'd received.

Val had told her she was nuts when Darien met with Dr. Norton to see if he'd give her the donor's information, which of course, he couldn't because it was anonymous. All he was able to tell her was the donor had been a healthy woman, and the organs had come from somewhere in the Midwest.

Darien had been cleared to drive after three months with a handicap tag on her car, which she wasn't pleased with, but she understood. Since she was getting back to a somewhat normal life, Val had finally made the tough decision to move out and let her go on her own.

As soon as Val was gone, Darien now had nothing to do and no one to talk to. She tried PTSD groups and veteran groups, but nothing helped the depression she was buried under. She finally began researching at the hospital where she'd had her surgery, checking with anyone who could give her organ transplant information. After nearly six weeks of getting nowhere, she finally found out that her donor organs had come from a hospital in Iowa City.

Darien rushed home and called the hospital, looking for information on a woman that would've died the night her donor organs had become available. It took her an hour to finally be directed to the person who could give her names of the three patients who'd passed away during the twenty-four hour time period. Two of them were women. After a quick Internet search, she was sure Paulette Sandinsky was not her donor, especially since she was eighty years old. That left one name: Janice Hoffman. There was no obituary listed, but Janice's name was affiliated with Hoffman Farm, an agriculture and dairy farm on the outskirts of Tipton, Iowa. Further research revealed that Tipton was a very small town of around 3,500 residents.

Darien took a deep breath and booked a flight and a rental car. Then, she found the only motel in Tipton and booked a room for a couple of nights. She sent Val a text message saying she thought she'd found her donor's family and was heading to Iowa.

***

The flight had gone by quickly and before she knew it, Darien was standing in the parking lot of the airport in Cedar Rapids, Iowa. The air seemed different. It smelled more like dirt than the salty tingle of the beach air she was used to. After signing the papers for her rental car, she made the hour long drive to Tipton.

The motel was small. She estimated there were no more than twenty rooms in the building. The older woman at the desk looked her over a few times. Darien knew she stuck out like a sore thumb. Everyone around her was in jeans or jean shorts and some form of boots. She'd worn jeans, but the sneakers on her feet screamed outsider.

"Where are you from?" the older woman asked.

"California," Darien answered.

"What brings you all the way to Tipton?"

"Oh, I'm on vacation, visiting an old friend."

"Well, here's your room key. Enjoy your stay," she said, walking back into the other room to continue watching the show playing on the TV.

Darien nodded and headed back outside. The number five was on her key, so she moved her car into the space in front of her room and walked inside with her bag. The room was small with a double bed, a microwave, and a mini-fridge. The décor was like something directly out of the sixties with drab green and gold coloring. She dropped her bag on the floor near the dresser and pulled the map from the side pocket that she'd printed before leaving her house. Her motel was circled in red pen with the Hoffman farm highlighted in yellow. It was too late in the day to make an unannounced visit, so Darien walked next door to the mom and pop style diner, where she ordered a chicken pot pie and a water to go.

Chapter 5

The next morning, Darien dressed in jeans, a new, light blue t-shirt that was meant to look old and faded, and her sneakers. She covered her short hair with an old dark-blue ball cap with a surf logo on the front of it as she headed out to her rental car. She'd chosen to leave during brunch time so maybe she'd miss the early morning hustle and bustle of the farm. The streets were empty as she drove across town toward the rolling hills of the outskirts on the northern end.

Darien's heart raced when the cattle fence came into view. She was starting to wonder if Val had been right all along about this being a mistake as she drove past the gravel road that led to the tan-colored house. A large barn and smaller structure that looked like a horse stable were in the distance. A large building also sat on the opposite side of the property. Cows of all different colors were scattered around an open field on that side. She made another pass by the property before heading back into town to get some lunch at the diner she'd eaten at the night before.

Mustering her courage once again, she got into the car and headed back towards the farm. This time, she noticed an old sign near the gate that had the word

HIRING scrawled across it in black paint. She quickly turned in and drove up towards the house.

A ranchhand who looked about her age walked by as she was getting out of the car. He was wearing dusty jeans, an old t-shirt, and a worn pair of cowboy boots.

"You here about the job? Or are you lost?" he asked with a raised eyebrow.

Darien cleared her throat. "I…yeah, the job." She nodded, looking around, hoping it wasn't some kind of animal slaughtering or other unconventional farm work.

"Courtney's not here, but Beverly is in the house. Come on." He spit tobacco on the ground and kicked some gravel over it with his boot. "I'm Ernie, by the way. What's your name?"

"Darien."

"Where are you from?"

"West coast."

He nodded, pulling open the screen to the back door. "Ms. Beverly," he called.

"I'm in the kitchen, Ernie. Come on in."

Darien followed him into the two-story, ranch-style home to the kitchen, where an older woman with grayish brown hair was standing near the sink. She had a few extra wrinkles and slightly worn skin from the obvious years she'd spent in the fields of the farm. She plopped the dish towel over her shoulder and turned around.

"This is Darien. She's here about the farmhand job, and Courtney's out at the market, making a delivery."

"I'll take it from here," she said, nodding for Darien to come further into the room. "I'm Beverly Hoffman. Welcome to our farm."

"Thank you," Darien replied, wondering how this woman was related to her donor. The nervousness in her chest had started to subside, making her feel a little more comfortable in the stranger's home.

"What brings you out this way? You don't look like you're from around here," Beverly stated.

"You're right, I'm sure I stand out like a rooster in a hen house, but I'm a hard worker. I've been through a lot this past year and I came out here to clear my head and put the past behind me."

Beverly nodded. "I have some hot biscuits and honey. Would you like some?" she asked, pulling the towel off the hot food and sliding the plate over.

"Yes, ma'am. Thank you." Darien smeared a little of the fresh honey over the two biscuit pieces and pushed them back together, eating it like a sandwich.

"Did your momma ever tell you it's not polite to wear hats and sunglasses in the house?" Beverly chided.

"Oh, I'm sorry." Darien pulled her hat off and reached for the sunglasses, slowly pulling them down. "These are prescription. I'm afraid I left my regular glasses at home."

"You don't have to take them off on my account," Beverly said, stiffening when she saw a glimpse of Darien's bright colored eyes before she pushed the dark glasses back up. "Where did you say you were from?"

"Arizona." Darien grinned.

"That's a long way from Iowa." Beverly patted her hand. She was unable to figure out why she'd felt such a connection to the stranger, but there was something about her that Beverly liked. "Well, whatever you're running from, honey, you're safe here."

"Thank you. I'm recently out of the military, so I guess you could say that's it. I'm trying to find myself again."

"Our farmhand job doesn't pay a whole lot, maybe a dollar over minimum wage, and it's cash, under the table. It's hard work with long hours, mostly fixing the fence and doing other odd jobs. You may have to handle an animal occasionally."

"That's fine with me," Darien replied, finishing her biscuit. She'd ridden a horse a little as a kid, and she'd encounter donkeys, camels, and various chickens and roosters in the villages while on her three tours in Iraq and Afghanistan.

"Alright. Well, my son handles the dairy side of the farm, and my daughter-in-law, Courtney, pretty much runs everything else. She'll be the one to get you started, but she won't be back until later today. I have a little bit of a health issue, so my days of working on the farm ended a couple of years ago."

Darien nodded. "I'm sorry to hear that."

"Oh, I'm fine. Thank you, though." Beverly poured Darien a glass of freshly squeezed lemonade. "So, you're retired military, you said?"

"Correct."

"Maybe you can tell me some of your stories one day. I'm sure you have a bunch."

"They'd probably bore you to tears, but I'd be glad to." Darien wondered what it was about senior citizens and people that were ill, that made them enjoy hearing someone tell them a story. When she was going to the veteran's support and PTSD recovery groups, everyone had wanted to hear each other's stories. Everyone except her. The counselors had told her it would be beneficial for her healing if she talked, but she'd chosen to stay silent. There was something about being on the farm and talking with Beverly that made Darien want to tell her everything.

"Be back in the morning anytime before eight, ready to work. You might want to think about a pair of boots. I don't think those sneakers are going to hold up for long out in the field."

"Yes, ma'am." Darien smiled. She'd packed a pair of her desert tan-colored recon boots, so she'd planned on wearing them.

***

The next morning, Darien showed up at the farm just before eight, wearing her combat boots, jeans, and a dark blue t-shirt. Her ball cap was pulled down over her short hair, and her eyes were covered by the dark glasses she always wore.

"Morning," Beverly announced from her position at the screen door. "Nice boots."

Darien nodded with a smile.

"Courtney had to go into town to get my prescriptions refilled, but I told her I hired you. Ernie knows what she wants you to start with. He'll show you around. He's probably over in the barn somewhere."

"Yes, ma'am." Darien headed off in the direction she'd pointed and found the ranch hand working on a rotary tiller.

"Fucking piece of shit!" he spat, kicking the machine.

Darien cleared her throat and he spun around. "Sorry," he grimaced.

"I'm ex-military. You can't say anything I haven't heard or said myself. What's the problem?" she asked.

"It won't start. I told Courtney it makes a better anchor than a tiller, but she doesn't want to spend the money to get a new one."

"Do you mind if I have a look at it?" "Have at it. When you've had enough, there are a couple of boards on the fence near the main road that need to be nailed back up. Any tools you need are in here in the barn, along with nails and new boards."

"Sounds like fun." Darien shook her head.

"We have a couple of goats and mini horses that keep knocking the boards down. Anyway, when you're done fixing the fence, you're supposed to start repainting it. The paint is over there in those five gallon buckets, along with the brushes. There are a couple of empty containers around here that are smaller if you want to transfer the paint a little at a time. That might be easier than carrying around the five gallon buckets."

Darien nodded and squatted next to the tiller when he walked away. She wasn't sure what she was doing on the farm. She'd come to thank her donor's family. Now here she was doing manual labor for pennies. Shaking her head, she stood to grab a pair of pliers and a screwdriver. Darien was drawn to the farm and to Beverly. She wasn't ready to give away her true reason for being there, so she sucked it up and went to work, cleaning out the carburetor on the gas-powered tiller. She had it running with no problem a few minutes later and moved on to the fence.

***

The sun bore down on Darien's back as she walked along the fence line, hammering the loose boards and making notes on a handmade map of the ones that needed to be replaced. Sweat beaded along her forehead, rolled down her back between her shoulders, and covered her abdomen. The Middle Eastern desert had been hot, but it was nothing like the humidity and blistering heat on the farm. She felt like she was melting into a puddle. Darien pulled the front of her shirttail up, revealing her toned body as she wiped the sweat from her face. She hadn't noticed the vehicle coming down the road until it skidded sideways, nearly missing the turn for the farm. She was on the far end of the fence line along the main road, so she could barely make out the white truck and the driver who got out of it. Shrugging, she tucked her shirt back in and went back to nailing the boards.

Chapter 6

Courtney climbed out of the truck, shaking her head. She couldn't believe she'd not only missed the driveway entrance, but she'd nearly crashed through the fence. The fence that stranger with the impeccable body was working on. She shook her head. She knew the worker Beverly had hired was female, but she'd never seen a body like that on another woman. The sculpted midriff made her warm in places she'd hadn't thought about in almost a year.

"Here's your medicine," Courtney called out as she walked inside.

"Wonderful," Beverly replied, coming down the stairs slowly.

"We should set you up in the bedroom that's down here."

"Nonsense," Beverly huffed. "I'll use the same bedroom I've had for the last forty years until I can't walk anymore."

Courtney shrugged.

"Did you meet Darien yet?"

"No. I'm pretty sure I saw her though."

"Oh, she's as sweet as can be. She's very quiet though. As a combat veteran, I'm sure she has her reasons." Beverly poured a glass of lemonade. "Anyway, Ernie said she fixed the tiller."

"Really? I was about to replace that old piece of shit." Courtney poured her own glass and sighed. "I still don't like the idea of a stranger working here. I was going to hire Mr. Miller's son to do the handy work."

"Darien is cheap labor and she's probably the hardest worker this ranch has ever seen. I'm sure she'll do just fine."

"She drives a rental car and you're paying her under the table, minimum wage at that. Did you even see her ID? Where's she from? What's she doing here?"

"I didn't need to, dear. All of that is none of my business anyway. I trust my instincts and something tells me that woman is a lost soul looking for a home. By fixing that old dilapidated tiller, she's already saved us some money, so quit bitching and go introduce yourself to her."

Courtney smiled and drank her lemonade before heading out to the barn in search of Ernie. She was nearly mowed down when Darien walked out with a pile of fence boards up on her shoulder.

"Whoa," Courtney screeched, ducking before the long boards took her head off.

"I'm sorry." Darien stepped to the side. "I didn't see you there." In all honesty, she hadn't seen the beautiful woman because her peripheral vision was nothing but darkness. Darien was a little surprised that she hadn't heard her footsteps though.

Courtney eyed the woman in front of her up and down. She was definitely the person standing near the fence showing her bare torso to the passing cars. She was a little taller than Courtney and lean with slightly broad shoulders. Her clothing gave way to the subtle curve of feminine hips and small breasts, but other than that, she was the type of woman Courtney had only read about in the fiction novels she read. She definitely screamed lesbian. In fact, it was so obvious that it could've been tattooed on her forehead. Still, Courtney let her eyes linger a little longer. She'd only ever been attracted to women like herself—country and farm-raised, but still feminine enough to keep you guessing which team she batted for.

"I'm Darien Hollister, the new farmhand," the woman said, breaking Courtney's concentration.

Courtney mentally chided herself for staring at the good-looking stranger. The last thing in the world she needed to do was send mixed signals to someone who would never have the chance to be with her. It wasn't the butch factor. No, that was a newfound interest apparently, as Courtney found it hard to pull her eyes away. No, she was and always would be, someone else's girl. That's what Courtney had said the day the ring was put on her finger and she said I Do, five years earlier.

"Courtney Hoffman," she mumbled.

"It's nice to meet you," Darien replied, trying desperately not to stare at the beautiful woman in front of her.

Courtney had tanned skin, pretty green eyes, and wavy, light brown hair that hung down past her shoulders with dirty blonde highlights from the long days in the sun. She was a little shorter than Darien and had a slim build with nice curves. She was wearing a white tank top, cut-off jean shorts, and ankle length, slip-on cowgirl boots.

Courtney couldn't see Darien's eyes through the dark lenses of her sunglasses, but she was sure she'd just been given the once over. Beverly's new hire was going to be trouble, she could feel it. She cleared her throat and said, "I'm assuming since you have those boards, Ernie gave you my instructions."

"Yes, ma'am. I found five that were missing or too rotten to nail back up, so I'm working on replacing them now," Darien replied.

Courtney nodded. "Did he tell you about painting the fence too?"

"Yes, ma'am."

Courtney smiled and shook her head. "You don't have to call me ma'am. Courtney will do just fine. Ernie will help you if you need anything. Otherwise, I'll be in the crop field or the house."

Darien smiled and nodded before walking away and heading down the driveway towards the stretch of fence she was working on. "What the hell am I doing here?" she muttered to herself as she wiped the sweat from her face for the hundredth time that day. She still couldn't figure out why a quick trip to say thank you had turned into her taking a manual labor job for next to nothing. She shook her head.

Truth be told, her mind had become clearer in the last twenty-four hours than it had been in the last nine months. The sun had felt good on her skin, and the fresh air was almost addicting. Looking back towards the house, she felt a sense of sadness, knowing her donor, Janice, was the missing link in their family. She hadn't quite figured out the connection, but she was sure Janice was Beverly's daughter and probably Courtney's sister-in-law, since Beverly had described Courtney as her daughter-in-law.

Darien shrugged and went back to nailing the boards to the fence. She wasn't quite ready to face the bitter truth.

***

Later that afternoon, Darien carried one of the five gallon buckets and two brushes out to the main road and began painting the fence, one post and one board at time. The property was nearly fifty acres, so she estimated it taking her the better part of three weeks to get the entire thing painted, give or take a few days if she were to be pulled aside for other projects, like fixing machinery or replacing broken and missing boards along the way.

She made it a point to end her day early, so she wouldn't have to remove her sunglasses. Her new eye color was striking, and she knew it would give her away, leading to many questions that she didn't know the answers to. She quickly cleaned out the brushes and put the paint buckets off to the side in the barn before walking towards her car. Suddenly, a backfiring sound from a tractor in the distance sent her mind straight to the frontlines of war. Darien hit the pavement, scurrying for cover as she checked her flank and reached for her automatic rifle. The fading sound of her name being called in the distance, moving closer and closer, finally brought her back to reality. She hadn't had an episode that severe since she'd gotten her sight back; definitely not while she was awake. Most of her nights, however, were still riddled with bad dreams.

"Are you alright?" Ernie asked.

Darien turned her head, looking for the voice. "Yeah," she sighed, seeing Ernie come into her line of sight.

"Beverly mentioned you were a veteran. I guess you were in the war, huh?"

"Something like that," she sighed, forcing a fake smile.

"Well, have a good one. I'll see you in the morning," he replied, walking away.

Darien got into her rental car, pulled out of the driveway as the sun began to set over the rolling hills, and headed towards town. She wanted an ice-cold beer to calm her nerves and cool her from the hot sun, but she knew alcohol would only make her PTSD symptoms worse.

She rolled the window down, letting the fresh air in as she chuckled, thinking about how the rental car, gas, and motel stay were costing her nearly twice what she was being paid at her new job for the week. Therefore, it was actually costing her money to work at the farm. It certainly was unconventional, and completely out of the perfect box she'd built around her life, but for some unexplainable reason, being on the farm made her feel alive again.

Chapter 7

At the end of the week, Darien couldn't remember the last time she'd done so much manual labor for a job. She was worn out, but it felt good. The physically active job was better than going to any gym. She'd only seen Courtney a couple of times since all she'd been doing was working on the fence, while Courtney and Ernie tended to the agriculture crops. Darien had noticed a young guy at the house a couple of times, talking with Courtney, and assumed he was Beverly's son who managed the dairy side of the farm. He was also more than likely Courtney's husband. He stood a little too close for a co-worker, and lingered too long for a friend. The plain gold band on the ring finger of her left hand was a dead giveaway. Plus, Beverly had referred to Courtney as her daughter-in-law when they'd first met. As soon as Darien came in from the field for another large bucket of paint, Beverly invited Darien inside for lunch, which she politely accepted. A platter of sandwiches was sitting on the table next to a large pitcher of lemonade.

"How was your first week?" she asked, sitting down adjacent to Darien.

"Fine. Thank you, again."

Beverly nodded towards the plate. "Help yourself. They're turkey and ham with a few diffcrent kinds of cheese and brown mustard."

Darien smiled and grabbed one of the sandwiches.

"It has to be costing you more for that rental car and motel room than I'm paying you."

"How do you—"

"This is a small town, honey. There isn't much that gets past the folks around here," Beverly interrupted. "Anyway, we have a little apartment above the barn. There's not much to it—a sink, mini fridge, microwave, twin bed, stand up shower, couple of tables, and a ratty old sofa. Ernie used to rent it from us until he moved in with his girlfriend a few months ago. I think he left some dishes and utensils." She paused. "It's yours if you want it."

"How much?" Darien asked.

Beverly shook her head. "No charge. I can't pay you a higher wage, but I know how hard you work. Call it a bonus." She shrugged.

Darien thought about it as she ate her lunch. It would save her money for sure. The living conditions weren't exactly ideal, but she'd lived in much worse while on deployment. "Okay," she said, nodding her head.

"Great. Check out of the motel and return your rental car this afternoon. I'll have Ernie bring you back here."

Darien wasn't thrilled about having no transportation. If she decided she couldn't handle her secret any longer, she'd need a way to the airport, but she was wasting money on the car.

"I see the gears in your head turning," Beverly laughed softly. "Mr. Miller, down the road, has a slew of crap at his farm. He will probably sell you a vehicle if you feel the need to have one. Oh, and you can wash your clothes in our washer and dryer. There's not one in the apartment and the closest Laundromat is in town."

"Thanks. Do you mind if I take the rest of the day off to settle my affairs?"

"That's not a problem. I'll send Ernie for you in a few hours."

"My rental is from the airport in Cedar Rapids, so I'll return it and take a taxi back to the motel."

"Nonsense. He'll meet you at the airport in three hours."

Darien nodded with a smile. "Thank you for lunch, and well, for everything."

***

Darien's phone didn't get much of a signal at the farm. It was hit or miss most of the time, so she had to wait until she was back in town to call Val and give her an update. She decided to drive down to Mr. Miller's beforehand.

"Can I help you?" an old man asked. He'd seen the little white car coming down the road before it turned into his long driveway.

"Mr. Miller?" Darien asked, stepping out.

"Who's asking?"

Darien stuck her hand out. "Staff Sergea—" Darien cleared her throat. She still wasn't used to dropping her military title. "Darien Hollister. I'm a farmhand at Hoffman Farm up the road. I'm looking for a vehicle, and Beverly said you may be able to help me."

"Oh, she did?" He nodded, spitting tobacco on the ground. He looked down, noticing the recon boots on her feet. "You military?"

"Retired," she answered, noticing the wrinkled Navy anchor tattooed on his arm.

"I might have something around here for you. Come on."

Darien followed him as they walked around the side of his house to what Darien could only refer to as a car graveyard. Mr. Miller pointed to a large garage with five or six vehicles in it, mostly cars from the fifties and sixties with a pair of vintage, worn-out trucks in the middle.

"You can have one of those trucks for a thousand. They both run, just need a little TLC."

Darien nodded and walked around, looking at both of them, paying careful attention to one in particular. It was a little rusty with faded blue paint.

"That's a 1950 Ford F100. It came from the factory with a flathead V8 and a three speed column shift transmission, but my son replaced it with a straight six and four on the floor in the '80s when he was driving it to high school," he said, shaking his head.

"When's the last time you had it running?" Darien asked.

"Oh, my grandson and I mess around out here every now and then. I think we drove that one about six months ago."

"I'll be back tomorrow with the cash."

"Sounds good. I'll get my grandson to put some fresh gas in it and air up the tires for you. He's spending the summer here with us, so that'll give him something to do."

"Great. See you in the morning."

***

Darien made it to the bank just before closing time to withdraw the cash. Then, she headed to her motel where she packed up her suitcase and checked out at the front desk. On the way to the airport, she dialed Val's number.

"Hey, I was starting to worry about you," Val answered.

"I'm fine. Heading to the airport at the moment actually."

"Oh, that's great. So, you're heading home?"

"Not exactly. That's why I was calling. I've decided to stay longer."

"Did you meet the family?"

"I think so."

"You think? Darien, what the hell have you been doing all week?"

Darien cleared her throat. "Working on their farm."

"What?"

"My donor's family owns a dairy and agriculture farm. They were hiring when I drove up and assumed that's why I was here. I clammed up and said yes. Anyway, I'm renting an apartment over the barn and I don't get very good cell service out there. That's why I'm calling. You'll need to send me letters through the snail mail, or wait until I go to town and have service to check my voicemails and emails."

"Darien, are you sure you know what you're doing? This isn't like you. Working on a farm, really?"

"I don't know, Val. But I haven't felt whole in almost a year, and I can't explain it. Being here just feels right."

"Have you told your parents?"

"No. They won't understand. I'm going to send them an email and tell them I've decided to travel a bit, now that I have my sight back."

"How's that going by the way? Do you have enough of your medication?"

"I haven't had any vision problems, and yes, I have enough medication for six months," Darien replied.

"I still think this is a crazy idea, but if there's one thing I know about you, you're all in with everything you do. Just be careful and come home at the first sign of any vision problems. Don't forget what Dr. Norton told you."

"I know. There could be permanent vision changes, including complete vision loss, within the first year. You don't have to remind me, Val," Darien stated. Then she gave her the address to the farm and hung up the phone before she pulled into the airport.

***

Darien had stopped for take-out on the way to check out of the motel, so when Ernie picked her up, she had him take her straight to the farm. As soon as he was gone, she walked up the outdoor staircase that led to the apartment and walked inside, opening the windows to air out the small room. It was about the same size as her motel room, so she found it easy to get adjusted to her new surroundings as she unpacked her clothes and toiletries. She was surprised to find a small radio under the kitchen sink. She noticed the batteries were dead when she tried to turn it on. After looking around for a few minutes, she finally found an open package of batteries with four left, which was what she'd needed. She made a mental note to get another big pack when she went into town to get groceries. Then, she turned it on and adjusted the dial, finding two country stations and a rock and roll station that advertised music from the seventies and eighties on its commercial. She left the radio tuned into the rock station and turned the volume up. If she didn't have TV, at least she could listen to some music.

Chapter 8

The next morning, Courtney watched out the window as Darien walked down the steps on the side of the barn and headed down the driveway. She checked her watch, noticing that it was nearly eight-thirty.

"If you want to know where she's going, all you have to do is ask her," Beverly chided.

"What?" Courtney moved away from the curtain in haste. "I don't care what she does. I still can't believe you're renting the apartment to her. Are you sure that's a good idea?"

"I don't see why not." Beverly shrugged. "Ernie lived up there for three years."

"Yes, but you knew Ernie." Courtney walked into the kitchen with her cup of coffee.

"What's really bothering you?" Beverly asked.

"Nothing. I'm fine. I'm headed to town to get a few things. Do you need anything?"

Beverly shook her head. "I'm feeling a little tired today. I think I'll lie down for a little while."

"I can stay. I'm not in dire need of anything. I was just going to replenish a few things that are running low."

"No, go on. I'll be fine," Beverly said, waving her hand at her.

Both women turned towards the window when they heard a low rumble in the driveway. Courtney moved the curtain aside and raised an eyebrow. "What the hell?" she murmured.

Beverly stepped closer. "Looks like Mr. Miller sold Darien a truck."

Courtney shook her head and moved away from the window quickly when Darien climbed out and headed towards the house. Beverly pulled the front door open before Darien had a chance to knock.

"Good morning," Darien said with a smile as she stood in the doorway with her sunglasses on. Her short hair was a little messy on top, but cropped neat around her ears and collar.

"Is that a Ford you got out there?" Beverly asked.

"Yes. A 1950 to be exact."

"Does it run okay?"

"I definitely need to give it a tune up and get some of the rust off the bed. Other than that, it's in good shape. That's actually why I came over. Do you know how I can get a hold of Ernie? I'm afraid the truck probably won't make it to town in the shape that it's in now, and I need to go to the automotive store to get the parts to work on it."

"You're in luck. Courtney was just about to go to town to do some shopping of her own. I'm sure she won't mind if you tag along. She can run to Carl's Auto. If he doesn't have what you need, he can order it for you," Beverly said.

"Oh, I wouldn't want to impose."

Beverly looked over at Courtney with a raised eyebrow.

Courtney cleared her throat. "I don't mind. Carl's is on the way to the market anyway."

"Oh, good. I need to pick up some groceries and batteries anyway, so that works out great." Darien smiled. "I'm ready to go when you are."

"Give me about ten minutes," Courtney replied, before going into the kitchen to refill her coffee cup.

"Maybe tomorrow I can hear one of those stories we talked about. If you're not too busy with the truck and everything, of course," Beverly said.

"Sure thing," Darien responded with a nod and walked back over towards the truck parked near the barn.

"This will give you two some time to get to know each other. Then, you'll see she's not the big bad scary stranger you think she is," Beverly muttered when Courtney walked back into the living room.

Courtney made sure Beverly made it back up the stairs to her room before storming off to find the reclusive farmhand.

***

They were halfway to town before Courtney finally said something to break the ice. Darien had been content with watching the fields and pastures full of rolling hills go by through the window and wasn't in the mood for twenty questions.

"Where are you from?" Courtney asked.

"Arizona," Darien mumbled. Her mind was going over everything she needed to get for the truck. She remembered the large tool chest in the barn and hoped it had everything she'd need inside.

"What are you doing in Iowa?"

Darien stared at the woman next to her through her sunglasses. She was young and beautiful and had stirred a mix of feelings in Darien that she forgot existed, but Courtney's obvious discontent for Darien made her ask herself the same question.

"Would you believe me if I said I didn't know?" Darien answered.

"It's not my place to believe you. I don't own the farm."

"You don't care for me much, do you?" Darien questioned.

Courtney shook her head. "I don't know you."

Darien sighed, "I can't tell you why I'm here because I don't know myself. I need a change of scenery and this is where I wound up."

Courtney turned into the parts store parking lot and rolled to a stop near the front. "I have to go next door to the farm supply store, so I'll meet you back out here when I'm finished. Then, we'll head over to Wal-Mart. They should have everything you need for the apartment or whatever."

***

Darien was on the lowered tailgate of Courtney's midsize truck, with her legs crossed at her ankles and a repair manual open in her hands. Courtney couldn't quite figure out the mysterious woman and that bothered her. The unwelcoming, intense physical attraction had also put her on edge. She had no idea why she was so drawn to this stranger.

"Are you ready?" Courtney asked.

Darien couldn't see the woman standing nearby until she turned her head to face her head on, but she'd heard the distinct staccato of shoes on the asphalt.

"Whenever you are," Darien answered, hopping down and closing the tailgate.

Courtney stayed silent as she drove a little further down the road to the large retail store that had become Tipton's general store a few years back. She parked the truck and they walked inside together, separating as soon as they were inside.

Darien had been in Wal-Mart enough over the years to know exactly where she was going. She grabbed a cart and headed towards electronics to get a large pack of batteries. Then, she went over to the home goods area to find a laundry basket, bed sheets, a couple of towels, a toaster oven, and a small coffee pot. From there, she passed by the clothing where she grabbed a couple of shirts along with socks and a package of underwear.

After she had the necessities, Darien walked across the store to the grocery side, grabbing a few things here and there, when she ran into Courtney, who eyeballed everything in her cart like a mother hen.

"You can take those off inside," she scolded, pointing to Darien's sunglasses.

"They're prescription." Darien shrugged.

Courtney turned away with her basket and called over her shoulder, "Don't buy any vegetables. We have whatever you need fresh on the farm. If Beverly finds you eating veggies from a chain store, she's liable to run you over with that old truck of yours."

As she walked away, Darien watched her ass move under the cut-off shorts she seemed to always wear.

Then, she rolled her eyes and took the vegetables out of her cart.

***

When they got home, Darien donned her hat and changed into a dark blue tank top with a black sports bra under it to go with the jeans and sneakers she was already wearing. Then, she turned her little battery-powered radio up loud on an old rock and roll station and spent the rest of the day out in the hot sun, working on her truck next to the barn.

By the end of the day, she'd changed the plugs, plug wires, oil, oil filter, and radiator fluid, and had also put a cleaning solution in the gas tank. She leaned against the side of the truck, pulling her shirt up to wipe the sweat from her face as she thought about all of the things she still had to do—change the distributor cap and points, clean the carburetor, then start sanding the rust spots on the bed so she could repair them. All of which she had planned for the next day.

***

"You're steaming up the window," Beverly teased when she saw Courtney looking out.

"What?" Courtney shook her head.

"I'm sure she'll let you help if you ask."

"The last thing I want to be doing is working on an old piece-of-shit truck."

"What's gotten into you lately?" Beverly asked.

"Me? What's gotten into you? I'm starting to think we need to take you back to the doctor."

"What for? I'm fine. I see him every three months like I'm supposed to. There are no new symptoms," Beverly stated. "I'm not the one moping around like a grouchy cat in heat."

Courtney's eyes nearly bugged out of her head. She had no idea what to say to the older woman sitting on the couch. They'd grown close over the years and were as close as mother and daughter, but she felt a little uncomfortable discussing her sex life with her mother-in-law.

"By the way, I invited her to lunch tomorrow," Beverly added.

"Is this turning into a weekly occurrence?" Courtney asked.

"I don't know. What is she bothering you so much about her? I don't think I've ever seen you this edgy."

"I don't know, Beverly. There's something about her. I can't quite put my finger on it."

"I think you're attracted to her and it's sent your head into a tailspin. Honey, it's okay to move on with your life."

Courtney sighed. "That's not it. She's—"

"A fine-looking specimen, if I do say so myself. Don't kid yourself or me." Beverly winked.

"Is that why you hired her? You're trying to set me up?" Courtney squeaked.

"Of course not," Beverly laughed. "What you do with your life is your own thing. You needed help around here and she looked willing and able. I think something inside of her is broken and she's come here to mend it. Cut her a little bit of slack and you might see she makes a great friend. We can always use friends in our life."

Courtney nodded and looked back towards the window.

Chapter 9

Darien had finished with the distributor cap and points, plus cleaned the carburetor by lunchtime. She quickly washed up and headed over to the house for lunch with Beverly.

"Come on in," Beverly called, seeing her in the doorway. "I know you've been working hard out there, so I told her to make something filling. I hope you like chicken and dumplings. Courtney's getting better and better with my recipes, so lunch should be divine."

Darien smiled and nodded at the older woman before following her into the kitchen.

"You know, I don't think I've heard you take a break in hours," Beverly added.

"I'm sorry if I've made too much noise," Darien replied.

"Oh, nonsense. I think I'd like to go for a spin when you get that old thing running." Beverly smiled.

"Sure," Darien murmured with a nod. She kept her sunglasses on, but she still saw Courtney's stare from across the room.

"Here you go, ladies. Enjoy," Courtney said, setting two bowls on the table.

"Are you not eating?" Darien asked.

"No, not right now. I'm going to take some over to Jason while it's hot. He was up all night with a cow that was giving birth."

Darien grimaced.

***

After they finished their meal, Beverly asked Darien to help her up the stairs. Darien knew something was ailing the older woman, but she wasn't exactly sure what is was. She'd noticed right away that Courtney was also living in the family house with Beverly and presumably, her caretaker.

"Would you mind telling me one of those stories?" Beverly asked as she began to get situated in her bed.

"Sure. What kind of story would you like?"

Darien moved to grab the small, wooden chair on the other side of the room. It literally felt like her heart had stopped breathing when she saw the framed photo on the dresser. She froze, looking into the same eyes that she saw everyday in the mirror. The picture was of a young woman with long blonde hair and a thin smile. She looked a little bit like a younger version of Beverly. There was no doubt in Darien's mind that this was Beverly's daughter, Janice, and her organ donor. The bright, bluish-green eyes of the woman in the photo were identical to hers. Darien quickly recovered and brought the chair over next to the bed.

"Oh, I don't know. Tell me how you wound up in the military," Beverly replied, finally getting herself comfortable enough to take a nap.

Darien pursed her lips. "I'm afraid that one is a little boring, actually."

"I'll be the judge of that." Beverly smiled.

Darien stretched her legs out in front of her, crossing them at her ankles. "Well," she began. "I was a modest student in school and when I graduated, I was offered a small academic scholarship. It paid for me to go to the local community college for two years, where I received an Associate in Applied Science degree in Criminal Justice." Darien paused. "I wanted to be a cop, at least until Career Day. The college invited a large group of companies, corporations, municipalities, and the military, to an annual gathering for students to help them choose a career path. I walked around each of the booths, paying close attention to what the local and state police had to offer. Then, on my way out, I passed by the military booths where a man in a Marine Corps uniform stepped in front of me. He asked my name and my major. Then he began telling me about the Marines and what they could do for me. I was already physically fit from playing sports and being generally active most of my life, and I was an only child who grew up with strict discipline from a father who'd work hard all of his life to provide for his family.

Darien uncrossed her legs and shrugged. "At the end of the day, the Marines sounded a hell of a lot better than the Phoenix Police Department. So, I started learning everything I could about the Marines, and when I graduated six months later, I enlisted."

"Wow, so you were a Marine! That's impressive, Darien. What did your parents think?" Beverly asked.

"Neither of them were happy at first, but they'd known for years that I was looking for a well-structured and disciplined career path. I was different from most kids and they accepted who I was from the very beginning. When I graduated from boot camp, they both said it was the proudest day in their lives, which meant a lot to me since being a Marine meant so much more to me than my high school diploma or the college degree that I'd earned," Darien answered as she watched Beverly's eyes slowly close.

She waited a few minutes before pulling the thin blanket up a little higher on the sleeping woman, then headed towards the stairs.

"Can we talk for a second," Courtney said from her position in the doorway of another bedroom down the hall, startling Darien since she hadn't seen the woman in her peripheral vision.

"Sure," Darien sighed. She thought she was getting used to the missing portion of her sight, but she was still caught off guard almost daily.

"I know Beverly's a curious person, but please don't tell her horrible stories about the war. They will give her nightmares."

Darien stiffened. "I'd never do that," she exclaimed. "No one should know what it's truly like over there," she murmured as she walked away.

**

Courtney watched her go down the stairs and out of the house. Then, she moved to the window, following Darien with her eyes until she disappeared into the apartment. Courtney had no idea what it was about the mysterious woman that both aroused and irritated her. She'd been listening at the door during Darien's story and was equally surprised that she'd been a Marine. Her work ethic and general nature were starting to make more sense.

Courtney closed the curtain and went to Beverly's room to check on her. She found the older woman sound asleep with her throw blanket pulled up. She seemed comfortable, so Courtney turned away, leaving her to nap. She saw the picture on the dresser and paused for a minute, letting her eyes linger over the face staring back at her, before going back downstairs.

Chapter 10

The next two weeks had slipped by in a blur. Darien had finally finished the dreadful fence painting and had been instructed to paint the barn, another daunting task that would take a couple of weeks to complete. She was starting to wonder if the manual labor was worth it. She was fairly certain that Beverly was sick and if Janice truly was her daughter, she wondered if telling her the truth was the right thing to do. There was no way she could ask what was wrong with the ailing woman. In a way, she didn't want to know. Seeing the picture of Janice on her dresser had made everything real, reminding her of the reason she was there to begin with.

Darien was at a crossroads and thought of packing her bags in the middle of the night more than once. Courtney had continued to keep her distance, while also keeping a watchful eye on the farm hand, something Darien was very much aware of. She couldn't figure out what Courtney's problem was with her. She tried to think of something she may have done to rub her the wrong way, but they'd never really had a confrontation, so she was at a loss as to why the young woman didn't like her.

***

At the end of her third week on the farm, Darien wanted to do nothing, except rest. Leading a battalion unit through the desert in the middle of a war zone hadn't required this much physical labor. She was in impeccable shape, but completely unaccustomed to moving all of her muscles at once until she was dead on her feet every day.

She slept nearly two hours past the sunrise on Saturday morning and stretched languidly before getting up to make a cup of coffee. Her stomach began to growl when the smell of dark roasted beans permeated the air. She turned on the burner of an old camping stove she'd found in the barn the week before and prepared a couple of eggs to scramble as she popped some precooked sausage into the microwave.

The sun was shining brightly in the cloudless sky when she looked out the window. She was about to turn back to her food when she saw Courtney walk out of the house with two large, black garbage bags, which she loaded into the back of her truck. She disappeared into the house and returned a minute later with a third bag, which she added to the others before driving away. Darien cocked her head to the side, wondering what the irritable woman was up to, before going back to her breakfast.

As soon as Darien finished eating, she moseyed over to the house with her second cup of coffee in her hand and knocked on the front door. It took Beverly a little longer than normal to answer the door, which meant she'd probably been upstairs.

"I didn't wake you, did I?" Darien asked.

"Nah. This old bird is up with sun on most days. Come on in." Beverly smiled.

"It's turning into a beautiful day, so I came over to see if you'd like to take that ride," Darien stated, before taking a sip of her coffee and stepping inside.

"Oh, I'd love to." Beverly smiled. "You have impeccable timing. This day didn't start out very bright, but you've definitely turned it around."

"Wonderful." Darien grinned.

***

The old truck sputtered to life a few minutes later and they drove away. Beverly pointed out all of the old farmhouses that were still around from when she was a kid as they rumbled down the country roads. As they moved away from the farmland, towards town, she pointed out the places where she'd gone to school and what had once been the house she'd grown up in, which was now a church. She told Darien the story about how the church had purchased her family's plot of land and dinky little house when her parents passed away a number of years ago. That property was now home to the largest church in Tipton.

After circling town, they stopped off for an ice cream cone at a small mom and pop parlor that purchased all of their dairy products from the Hoffman Farm and had been doing so every since the farm opened in the '40s.

"Were you ever married?" Darien asked when they got back into the truck.

"Boyd Hoffman was the best looking boy in my high school, in my opinion anyway. He had sandy blonde hair and incredible blue eyes. His family owned and operated Hoffman Farm. The summer before our junior year of high school, I got a job out at the farm working with the cattle. Boyd and I had already known each other from school, but we spent a lot of hours together that summer, working side-by-side from sun up to sun down. We fell in love and were pretty much inseparable after that." She smiled. "We had two wonderful kids together, before he died in a hunting accident."

"He sounds like a wonderful man. I'm sorry to hear that he passed."

"Life goes on as they say. What about you?" Beverly asked. "I won't insult you by asking if you have a husband. It is the twenty-first century after all, and I'm up with the times."

Darien smiled. "I've been single for as long as I can remember. I'm afraid the military life doesn't fit everyone," she replied.

"What about now, since you're retired?"

"I haven't been retired long, and I've sort of been taking the time to learn to how be just Darien, not Darien the Marine."

"That's understandable."

When Darien turned the truck into the long driveway, she noticed a large red pickup parked near Courtney's smaller white one. She'd barely rolled to a stop in her parking space near the barn when Courtney bolted from the house with a slightly taller man behind her.

"Oh, my God!" Courtney yelled. "I've been running around frantic, trying to find you!"

"Mom, where have you been?" the man said angrily. "And who is this?"

"Calm down, both of you. Jason, this is Darien Hollister, the farmhand I told you about. It's a beautiful day, so we took a drive," Beverly stated.

"You can't just take off without telling someone," Courtney snapped, biting back the tears. "I was worried to death that something happened to you."

"I don't like you going off with some stranger, mom. We don't know this woman. What if something had happened?" he said, eyeing Darien with a cold stare.

"I'm fine," she replied, sounding slightly winded.

"Come on, let's get you into the house where it's cool." Courtney grabbed Beverly's arm and helped her inside.

"I don't know who the hell you think you are, but you stay away from my mother. By the way, Courtney's my girl, don't you forget that," Jason spat before getting into his truck and driving away quickly, sending gravel flying.

Darien shook her head at the catastrophe the day turned out to be. She thought about packing her stuff and leaving without saying another word. She'd even taken her suitcase out and sprawled it open on the bed, but she felt too strong of a connection to the farm, to Beverly…and to Courtney. She couldn't simply cut ties and leave. She sat on the sofa and kicked her feet up on the rickety coffee table as Jason's words bounced around inside of her head. She knew he was married to Courtney, so she didn't understand why he felt the need to add in the additional warning.

***

Darien avoided the house for the next couple of days. Ernie instructed her on everything else that needed to be added to her to-do list, meaning Courtney had been avoiding her as well.

On Wednesday morning, Beverly spotted Darien coming out of her apartment and quickly opened the front door, calling her over. Darien obliged and crossed the short distance from the barn to the house, where Beverly asked her to come over for lunch and perhaps tell her another story.

Darien spent the rest of the morning listening to the music blasting from her small radio, while replacing the double belts on the walk-behind seeder. She had to take the thing apart completely to put the new belts on, then figure out how it went back together. There was no wonder why Ernie had left her with the task. She'd proven to be more mechanically inclined than anyone else on the farm so far, which meant she was given the difficult jobs on top of the mundane handyman work she'd been doing since she'd arrived.

As soon as it was noon on her watch, she washed her hands in the barn sink, then headed over to the house for lunch with Beverly. She was just about finished with the seeder. The dirt on her pants could attest to the difficulty of the job. Courtney eyed Darien up and down suspiciously when she walked inside. She was wearing her recon boots, jeans, a tight red t-shirt, and her sunglasses.

"She'll be down in a minute," Courtney said, setting the lunch plates on the table, before walking back to the counter to get the glasses for the pink lemonade.

Darien watched her moved around, trying hard to keep her eyes off the tan legs running from the bottom of

Courtney's cut-off shorts to the top of her cowgirl boots. She nearly fell out of her chair when Courtney stepped closer, reaching for her sunglasses.

"You have some dirt on your face," Courtney explained, pointing to her cheek. She was slightly shocked when Darien snatched away from her so quickly, almost like Courtney's touch would burn her or something.

All through lunch, Courtney watched the interaction between Darien and Beverly. It was like they'd known each other for years as they talked about topics from the weather to the upcoming town elections. Then, Beverly asked Darien to come up and tell her another story before heading to her room. Courtney shook her head as she watched them walk away. Then, she cleared the table and washed the lunch dishes before going back to work in the crop field.

*** *

"So, what would you like to hear about today?" Darien asked.

"Why don't you pick up where you left off with the last one?"

Darien thought for a minute. "After I enlisted, I headed off to basic training at Parris Island in South Carolina." She shook her head. "I thought I was going to die. I was in pretty good shape to start with and they still whipped my butt. I think I threw up more during those twelve weeks than I have in all of my life, especially during The Crucible. That's a fifty-four hour training course where you're sleep and food deprived. You cover about forty-five miles as you endure the worst hell imaginable while putting all of your training to the test."

Beverly laughed. "That doesn't sound like much fun."

"Oh, it definitely wasn't fun. I can assure you. But the day I put on that uniform and was addressed as 'Marine' for the first time was a very proud moment in my life. See, you're not a Marine until you make it through boot camp. Until then, you're simply a recruit." She smiled, thinking back to that day. It seemed like a complete lifetime ago.

"What kind of job did you do?" Beverly asked.

"Well, at that point, you're assigned your first rank, which is Private and first MOS. This is your Marine Occupation Specialty. It's based on test scores, education, and so on. Remember, I have a two-year college degree in Criminal Justice. Well that, along with my test scores, made me a prime candidate for military police, but I asked for Ground Combat instead, which is more commonly known as infantry. From there, I went through the ITB at Camp Geiger in North Carolina, which is infantry training school. That was fifty-nine days of more hell, but it's where I learned the skills that led me down an amazing and honorable career path."

"You definitely didn't have a desk job then." Beverly smiled.

"No," Darien laughed. " I took the Light Armored Vehicle course after infantry training, and that's where I became an LAV Crewman, which is basically someone inside of an armored vehicle. I was stuck on the east coast because the Marine Corps makes all female recruits go through basic training at Parris Island. So, because I did basic there, I was sent to Geiger for ITB. Once I'd finished LAV training, I was stationed at Camp Lejeune in North Carolina and assigned to an LAV Reconnaissance Battalion. I spent a year there training with my new unit, running drills and learning everything I could. That year was one of the hardest. You're basically a peon for the first nine months as you go from the rank of Private to Private First Class." Darien felt proud of all she'd accomplished as she talked about the early days of her life as a Marine.

"Early into my second year," she continued. " I was moved up in rank to Lance Corporal and went on my first deployment to South America, where I spent eight months in Columbia aiding in anti-drug operations which were mostly border patrols. We drove all over creation doing those recon patrols."

"That must have been interesting," Beverly said.

"It was boring as hell," Darien laughed. "We did have a couple of hair-raising moments while aiding in take-downs, but we were mostly there to train the local forces on how to stop the drugs coming across the border." Darien watched as Beverly's eyes began to close. "I'm going to leave you alone to take your nap. I need to get that seeder put back together before Ernie has a fit."

Beverly smiled and closed her eyes as Darien left the room. Darien didn't want to tell her story at first, but over the past few weeks, she'd starting feeling different. Talking to Beverly was helping her get everything off her chest that had built up for the past thirteen years. She'd never really talked to anyone about her time in the military and it was like a weight was slowing being lifted off of her. Her story was one she was proud of and should've been proud to tell, and Beverly was allowing her to finally see that.

Chapter 11

The next morning, Courtney sat down across from Beverly at the table with a cup of coffee and a bagel with cream cheese.

"Is that all you're eating for breakfast?" Beverly asked.

"I ate some bacon too."

Beverly shook her head. "No wonder you stay so skinny."

Courtney laughed. "I'm skinny because I sweat my ass off working long hours on this farm."

"I hired Darien so you wouldn't have to do so much, but it seems like you've been working even harder in the past month. I know for a fact that having her here has helped out a lot."

"I won't deny she's been a big help." Courtney bit into her bagel to end the sentence. She wasn't ready to talk about Darien. She couldn't seem to get away from the good-looking farmhand, no matter how hard she tried. "What do you talk about when she comes up to your room?"

"She tells me stories about her military days. Did you know she was a Marine?"

"Yes." Courtney set her bagel down. "She's not talking about being in the war, is she?"

"We haven't gotten to that yet."

"I need to get to work. I have a couple of bushels of carrots to harvest today." Courtney grabbed the half-eaten bagel from her paper plate and shoved it in her mouth as she tossed the plate into the trash.

Darien was coming down the steps from the apartment when Courtney walked out the front door of the house.

"Good morning," Darien said loudly, giving her a slight wave as she rounded the corner.

Courtney watched her open the large bay door of the barn and chided herself for ogling the woman before walking the opposite direction towards the field.

***

A few days later, Darien spent another two hours in Beverly's room, telling her about how she had spent the next year as a Lance Corporal, honing her skills as a marksman, while also moving through each job of her MOS, from being an LAV driver, to a scout, and a gunner. She'd also proven her leadership skills by leading a small group of Private and Private First Class ranked Marines through various training drills.

At the end of the year, she'd put in for a transfer to Camp Pendleton and after six months, it had been approved. As soon as she'd moved back across the country, she deployed for another six-month stint with her new recon battalion, this time in Kaneohe, Hawaii, where she worked with her unit doing combat readiness drills. At the end of the six months, she'd proven herself and her leadership abilities enough to be promoted to

Corporal, which was a junior non-commissioned officer. She'd also finished her third year as a Marine.

As soon as Darien had finished the next section of her story, she headed to her apartment since the sun was going down soon. She was barely inside when she heard a knock on the door. She quickly grabbed her sunglasses and walked over to the door.

"Can we talk?" Courtney asked, when Darien pulled the door open.

"Sure, come in." Darien stepped back, waving her arm for Courtney to enter the apartment. "Can I get you anything?"

"No. I came up here to ask you to stop with the stories."

"Why? Did Beverly say something?"

"No, but she doesn't have to. I think she's getting too attached to you."

"What?" Darien furled her brow. "That doesn't make any sense. She asked about life in the military, so I started telling her. She seems to enjoy our time and to be honest, it's done a hell of a lot for me. So, unless she's asked you to tell me to stop, I don't plan on it," she growled.

"Wow, are you really that self-absorbed? I knew you were bigheaded, but—"

"Why do you dislike me so much?" Darien asked, cutting her off. "You've treated me like the hired help since day one."

"You are the hired help!" Courtney snapped. "Which means you need to keep your ass outside working and not up in Beverly's room telling her stories to make yourself feel better!"

"Wow! Tell me how you really feel!" Darien snarled. "You're an arrogant bitch. Has anyone ever told you that?" She shook her head, stepping closer. "You think I'm self-centered? Have you even wondered why that woman is so interested in my life, or are you just too damn jealous that she's spending time talking with me to care?"

"How dare you!" Courtney shouted, moving closer. "You know nothing about any of us or our lives!"

"If you want me to know about you, then stop ignoring me," Darien murmured, closing the distance between them as her lips met Courtney's in a heated kiss, taking her breath away.

Courtney welcomed the taste of another woman's mouth on hers as she thread her arms around Darien's waist. She'd forgotten what is was like to be intimate and was starting to lose herself in the passionate kiss, until she remembered it was Darien touching her. She pulled away, backing up to put space between them as she stared at the dark sunglasses hiding Darien's eyes. She abruptly turned away, bolting from the apartment before Darien could say anything.

"That went well," Darien huffed as she removed the glasses and flopped down on the couch. "Manual labor, shit pay, kissing straight, married women. What the hell am I doing here?" she whispered. As therapeutic as talking to Beverly had been for her, she was starting to think coming to Iowa had been one huge mistake.

***

The next day was Saturday so Darien decided to stay as far away as she could get from anyone in the

Hoffman family. She left a little after ten that morning, heading into town to look for new jeans since hers were starting to look raggedy with paint stains and grease spots. She also needed to put some gas in her truck and pick up a few groceries. She stayed in town long enough to have the chicken pot pie special at the diner by the motel where she'd stayed when she first came to town.

When she arrived home later in the day, Courtney walked out of the house.

"Valerie Sherwin sent you something," she said curiously as she held the envelope out.

"Great," Darien smiled, taking it from her. "Thanks," she added before collecting her bags and heading up the stairs.

***

Courtney wondered who this Valerie person was as she watched her walk away. She neither had the time nor the patience to deal with her feelings. Kissing the stranger had been a huge mistake no matter how damn good it had felt. The fact that Darien had kissed her while getting strange letters from another woman was enough to make Courtney want to smack her. The last thing she needed was feelings for someone who was involved with someone else, and she didn't want the feelings to begin with.

"Has Darien ever mentioned Valerie in the stories she tells you?" Courtney asked, walking back into the house.

"No. Who is that?" Beverly questioned.

Courtney shrugged. "A letter arrived from her today for Darien."

77

"What was the address?"

"California, I think."

"She's single, if that's what you're getting at," Beverly said over the top of her reading glasses as she went through their mail.

"I...no. I don't care." Courtney huffed. "I was simply asking if you knew who it was. You two seem to spend a lot of time talking. I figured maybe she'd told you."

"Courtney, if you want to know, then ask her."

"It's none of my business." She got up and walked towards the kitchen. "What do you want for lunch?"

***

Darien put away her groceries and tore the tags off her new pants before hanging them in the closet. Then, she sat down on the couch and opened the letter from her cousin.

Darien,

How's life in the country? Have you told the family yet? Your parents keep asking me if I've talked to you. I'm assuming you're calling or at least emailing them when you get into to town and have cell service. Have you spoken to Dr. Norton? How is your vision? How much longer do you plan to stay out there? I'm sorry for all of the questions. It's been a month and your parents are worried about you. Hell, I'm worried about you. We all love and miss you. Write back soon.

Val

Darien wanted to write her back, but she didn't have anything remotely close to stationary, much less a stamp. She made a mental note to pick up both the next time she was in town and decided to walk over to the house to see if Beverly had any.

Courtney pulled the door open as soon as she knocked.

"Do you happen to have any stationary and stamps? I forgot to pick some up at the store," Darien asked.

Courtney was about to say no, but Beverly stepped up behind her.

"Hey, Darien. Come on in."

Courtney pushed the door wider and rolled her eyes as Darien walked inside.

"I'm sorry to bother you. I was hoping I could borrow some paper, an envelope, and maybe a stamp."

"Sure. It sounds like you're writing a letter." Beverly smiled and walked into the office, which was a room off the side of the living room.

"Replying to one, actually. My cell phone gets horrible service here, so I gave my family your address. I hope you don't mind."

"No, not at all," Beverly replied, handing her some paper, envelopes, and half a book of stamps."

"Oh, I won't need all of this."

"Sure you will. If not this time, then keep it to respond to the next letter you get." Beverly smiled. "Oh, how I miss the old days of getting a real letter in the mail."

"I'm kind of used to it from deployment. I didn't like talking to my family on the computer, so I always made them write to me."

"See, Courtney, some people are still old-fashioned."

Courtney nodded as she walked out of the room.

"Darien, I'd love to hear some more of the story later today. If you have time, of course."

"Sure. I need to get this letter done, then I'll be back."

Darien headed back to her apartment, where she sat on the couch and pulled the table close enough to lean over and use it as a writing surface.

Val,

Country life isn't what it's cracked up to be, that's for sure. My job involves a lot of manual labor: painting, fixing things, and so on. I haven't had much time to do much else, not that there is really a lot to do here anyway. I'm in kind of a rural area and the town itself isn't very big. They have two traffic lights and about 3500 people max.

As for the family, no, I haven't told them. Beverly, who is my donor's mother, is older, maybe 65-68 years old and ill. I'm not sure what it is. I don't have the heart to ask. I guess maybe I don't want to know if she's dying. That would be too much to handle. She's as sweet as can be. She likes to talk, or in my case, listen. She wanted me to tell her about my military life, which I wasn't willing to do at first, but it's been really therapeutic for me. I guess those therapists who kept telling me PTSD was real and talking about everything would help me get over the depression, must've been right after all.

I know I need to tell them the truth and why I'm here, but I'm being a little selfish because I know when I do, this will all be over, and I'm enjoying the connection, for now at least.

I need you to do me a favor and go to my place. (You should still have your key.) Send me any important mail and toss out the junk. I wasn't sure how long I'd be here, so I didn't set up a forwarding address. If you could check maybe once a week, that would be great. Also, I email my parents when I go to town, which isn't often, but I did send them one this morning. I know you're all worried about me, but I'm okay. I survived a living hell in Afghanistan. I think a little time on an Iowa farm will be fine. It's no cake walk though! Talk to you soon. My love to all of you. Miss you too, by the way!

Darien

She folded the paper and stuffed it into the envelope before addressing it and adding the stamp. Then, she walked down to the mailbox at the end of the road before heading up to the house.

Chapter 12

When Darien knocked on the door, Courtney let her in and pointed upstairs before closing the door. Darien shrugged, watching her walk away before she made her way up to Beverly's room.

"Knock knock," Darien said, standing outside of the door.

"Come in," Beverly said. She was already sitting up in her bed with the throw blanket pulled up over her legs. "Did you get your letter mailed?"

"Yes, and thank you again for the supplies."

"You're welcome." Beverly watched her grab the chair and bring it closer to the bed. "The sun will be going down soon," she sighed, looking through the opened curtains out the window.

Darien nodded, realizing she'd lost track of time, something that never happens. "I think the days go by faster the older I get." She smiled.

"Oh, you're still a spring chicken. Wait until you get to be my age, you're just glad to see each new one arrive," Beverly laughed.

Darien smiled again and shook her head. "So, where did I leave off last time?"

"I think it was the end of your first three years after you were in Hawaii."

"Oh, right. I'd just been promoted to Corporal and was taking on more leadership responsibilities as a junior NCO."

"Pardon my interruption," Beverly said. "I know you wear those glasses because of the prescription, but would you mind taking them off, just this once?"

Darien stiffened. Then, she took a deep breath and lowered her head as she pulled the dark sunglasses away. She set them on the nightstand next to her before slowly raising her eyes to Beverly.

Beverly inhaled sharply. She'd caught a glimpse of Darien's eyes once before when she'd first come to the house, but she wasn't at all prepared for the blow she felt as Darien's turquoise blue eyes locked onto hers.

"Are you okay?" Darien asked.

"Yes. I'm a little light-headed."

"Do you need me to get Courtney?"

The look of concern on Darien's face made Beverly smile. "No, dear. I'm fine." She sat up a little straighter. "I think I'd like to tell you a story today. If you don't mind."

"No, not at all," Darien replied.

"I told you Boyd and I had two wonderful children. You've met my son, Jason. That picture over there is my daughter, Janice. She was a hard-working woman, a good daughter, and a loving wife." Beverly wiped a tear from her cheek. "This past October, Janice went to town to run errands one afternoon, something she did quite often. I was in the kitchen making biscuits to go with our dinner that evening and Courtney was out in the back pasture with a couple of young mini horses that we were boarding." She paused to take a breath, then added,"

We haven't done any boarding this year." She looked up at Darien's eyes.

"Anyway, the tornado alarm wailed loudly, and I rushed out of the house towards the cellar. Ernie helped Courtney secure the animals in the barn, then we all rushed down inside together. We listened to the weather radio as they reported the twister touching down near SR 38 heading east. Then, it turned and went up Monroe for almost five miles, destroying Pickett Farm, before lifting up again. The report had it touching down two more times before disappearing out of our zone. Courtney and I climbed out of the cellar, thankful that the twister hadn't gotten close enough to cause any damage to our property. I went back inside to finish the biscuits, while Courtney fed all of the animals and Ernie continued seeding the new crops."

She paused to wipe another lone tear. "We'd forgotten all about Janice going to town earlier that day until a deputy from the Cedar County Sheriff's Office pulled into the drive. He said Janice's truck had been found twisted and mangled on the Pickett Farm. Eyewitness reports showed her vehicle traveling northbound on Monroe, presumably heading home from town, when the tornado warning sounded. She'd more than likely pulled off the road but had no way of knowing that she was in the direct path of the twister. The Picketts had come out of their cellar to a mass of destruction with a mangled, white vehicle in the middle of it."

Darien grabbed Beverly's hand.

"Mr. Pickett found Janice still inside the truck and badly injured. His neighbor had come over to make sure everyone was okay. The two of them got her out of the truck and drove towards town where an ambulance met them halfway. She was transferred to the ambulance, but the nearest trauma hospital was in Iowa City and she would never make it with the severity of her injuries. The ambulance met up with the Lifesaver helicopter a few miles down the road, and they transported her to Iowa City."

Darien held back her own tears. She'd known Janice had died, but she had no idea how tragic her death had been. She stared at the floor as Beverly finished.

"The deputy led the way as Courtney and I drove to Iowa City. When we arrived a half hour later, she'd already passed away on the operating table."

"Beverly, I'm so sorry," Darien murmured.

"Thank you. Courtney and I haven't had an easy time over the past seven months, but life goes on. I truly believe Janice is always here with us and you've shown me that. You remind me a lot of her with your dedication and work ethic. I think you and she would've been friends." She smiled and patted Darien's hand.

"I think you're right," Darien murmured, feeling closer to Janice and her family than ever before as the walls of her deceit began closing in on her. She was told by the therapists that any little thing could trigger her PTSD, making her feel suffocated.

"That's the first time I've ever told that story to anyone. I think it wore me out," she sighed, closing her eyes.

"Thank you for telling me," Darien whispered before leaving the room quickly with her sunglasses in her hand.

She took the stairs two at a time, rushing to get out of the house so she could breathe again. She looked up towards the door across the living room as she neared the bottom. Courtney caught sight of the familiar, bright eyes looking back at her and dropped the glass she was holding, which shattered to pieces on the hardwood floor. Darien rushed to clean up the glass.

Courtney stepped back and sat in a nearby chair for a second to collect herself. She felt like she'd just seen a ghost. After a few long breaths to calm her racing heart and settle the shock she'd just endured, she bent down to help Darien with the mess on the floor.

"You—" Courtney stared at the eyes looking back at her. "Your eyes...they're the same color as Janice's," she said softly.

"I know," Darien murmured, seeing the pain on her face.

Courtney furled her brow, looking slightly stunned.

"I saw the picture in Beverly's room. She told me it was her daughter, Janice," Darien stated as she finished cleaning up the glass.

Courtney watched her walk away without saying another word. Her mind was still reeling from the kiss they'd shared, and this was nearly enough to make her think she was losing her mind. She wondered how much Beverly had told Darien about Janice, or about any of them for that matter.

Chapter 13

Darien spent the next few days painting the white trim on the brown barn. She'd just about finished all of it by Wednesday and hadn't seen Courtney once since the broken glass on Sunday. Truth be told, she was glad she hadn't. She had mixed feelings when it came to Courtney. The younger woman was beautiful, but Darien was starting to feel much more than a simple physical attraction to her and that was a bad thing.

Darien walked into the barn to clean the paint brushes and put everything away, when she heard a noise like someone clearing her throat. She didn't see anyone since her peripherals were blacked out, so she turned her head in the direction of the sound.

Courtney was leaning against one of the posts with her hands shoved down into the pockets of her cut-off jean shorts and her booted feet crossed at the ankles. She was wearing a dark blue tank top and had her hair up in a makeshift bun with tendrils falling down.

"Can we talk?" Courtney asked, pushing off the post and looking up towards the apartment above the barn.

"I'm sorry. It was—" Darien set the stuff she was holding on the nearby bench. "I never meant for that kiss to happen. I—"

Darien was cut off by the rumble of a vehicle in the driveway.

"Courtney!" a male voice hollered.

"Jason?" Courtney murmured as she walked out of the barn.

"Hey, I figured you were out in the field," he said, walking over to her. "You want to go out with me tonight? I have two tickets to the rodeo," he added, throwing his arm around her shoulder.

"Jason, I can't. I'm sorry."

He followed the path of Courtney's eyes towards the barn when she stepped away.

"It's because of that farmhand, isn't it? I knew she was trouble," he spat as she stomped off towards the barn in search of Darien. He found her standing near the sink, washing out the paint brushes.

"What gives you the right to think you're a part of this family? You're a god damn farmhand," Jason yelled at her.

"Excuse me?" she replied, drying her hands on a nearby rag. "I'm not sure what's going on, but—"

"I want you out of here. You're fired as of right now. Go pack your shit and get off my property," he yelled.

Beverly had heard the commotion of him racing up the gravel driveway and calling out for Courtney, so she opened the front door to see what was going on.

"Now wait just a damn minute," Beverly shouted at him, stepping further outside. "How dare you talk to her like that," she continued. "First of all, I don't ever want to hear you talk to anyone that way again! Second, you have some respect for women. Your daddy raised you better than that. I'll smack your mouth! Darien is as much a part of this family as you are and don't you forget that! I still own this farm and she's not going anywhere!" she added, yelling louder as she started getting winded.

He stormed off to his truck, mumbling under his breath.

"I don't know what's gotten into you, boy," Beverly panted. "But, it…ends…now," she gasped, starting to collapse in the barn as he drove away.

Courtney and Darien rushed to her side together.

"She needs her medicine," Courtney said.

"I'll get her inside," Darien replied, as she bent down and picked up the frail woman.

As soon as Darien got her into the house, Courtney had Beverly's medicine waiting for her. She took it and started to relax a little bit as her blood pressure began to go back down and her constricted airway started to open up. Darien and Courtney waited a couple of minutes for the medicine to work, then they helped her up the stairs and into her bed. Darien walked away as soon as she was settled. When Courtney made her way back down the stairs, Darien was gone.

***

Darien was sitting on the couch in the apartment, trying to gather her thoughts when she heard a knock at the door. She'd known something was ailing Beverly, but she didn't know how bad it actually was until she witnessed the episode in the barn.

"Can I come in?" Courtney asked when Darien pulled the door open.

Darien nodded and moved to the side. Courtney walked in and sat down on the couch.

"Thank you for helping me with Beverly. She's…it's not easy sometimes," Courtney said softly.

Darien sat down next to her on the small sofa. "It's no problem. She's a special person. I'd do anything for her."

"She has Lupus," Courtney sighed. "It's effecting her heart and lungs more than anything, and it keeps progressing. A year ago, she was still working in the field for a few hours every day, but now, she's so tired she can barely walk up and down the stairs anymore."

Darien held back the tears that were burning her eyes. "I'm sorry," she murmured.

"Thank you. We take it one day at a time. Losing Janice really sent her downhill, but I've seen happiness in her eyes again since you arrived."

"She's brought a little happiness back into my life too. Like I said, she's a very special person."

"I'm sorry for trying to stop the stories. She's fragile and I'd do anything to protect her."

Darien nodded.

Courtney looked around. "I meant to tell you the other day, I like what you've done with the place. Ernie sort of threw stuff wherever and however," she added, changing the subject.

"Blame it on the military." Darien grinned.

"Actually, about the other day—"

"I'm sorry about that. The kiss was a simple misunderstanding and I apologize."

Courtney shook her head. "First of all, we were both involved. That kiss wasn't one-sided," she sighed, putting her hand on Darien's cheek. "There's no need to apologize." She squeezed her eyes closed and pulled her hand away as she stood to leave. She needed to go check on Beverly before her racing libido got the best of her. She was finding it harder and harder to control herself around the farmhand.

Darien got up to walk her out. "I know you're married, and I don't want to cause anymore problems. If you want, I'll go talk to Jason myself and clear things up," she said, holding the door as Courtney walked out onto the stairs.

Courtney looked back at her. "Don't worry about Jason, he's a pompous ass," she replied, shaking her head as she walked down the stairs.

Darien stood there with a questioning look on her face, watching Courtney's long hair blow in the wind and her ass sway under the cut-off shorts as she crossed the driveway towards the house.

***

The next morning, Courtney asked Darien to help Ernie tend to the crops so she could take Beverly into town to see her doctor. The older woman was still very weak from the day before and was having a hard time getting around. Darien had helped Courtney get Beverly into the truck, then she watched them drive away before heading out to the field, spending the rest of her day picking vegetables.

Chapter 14

The doctor made an adjustment to Beverly's medication and it had taken her the better part of two days to gather enough strength to get around on her own again. Each time her disease kicked in full-force, she had a setback and never fully recovered to the point she was at before the attack. Courtney hated watching her wither away, but she was happy to see a smile on her face again.

"What would you like for breakfast?" Courtney asked.

"Oh, I don't care. The doctor said I need to eat more oatmeal, but between you and me, it gives me the shits."

Courtney laughed. "Alright, how about an egg white omelet? I can throw in some fresh veggies and low-fat cheese."

"That sounds delicious," Beverly replied, moving to get out of her bed.

"Do you think you're strong enough to tackle the stairs?"

Beverly thought about it for a second. "Yeah, I'll be fine. Exercise is good for me."

"Okay." Courtney nodded.

"Will you please ask Darien to come see me when you head outside for the day?"

"Sure. I'll bring your breakfast up in a bit."

***

When Courtney found Darien, she was working on her latest job assignment, digging the trench for the irrigation piping in the new section Courtney and Ernie had added to the crop field.

"Beverly is feeling a lot better today. She wants to see you," Courtney said.

"That's good. I'll go up when I finish this line," Darien replied, removing her sunglasses to wipe the sweat from her face.

Courtney stole a quick glance at those beautiful, familiar eyes before shaking her head and walking away to start her own work for the day. She still couldn't get past Darien and Janice having the same eye color, but that was the only area where they were similar. In fact, both women were nearly the exact opposite of each other, which was why Courtney couldn't figure out why she was so attracted to Darien. She barely knew the woman because she avoided talking to her on most occasions, but they didn't need to talk to communicate. She was pretty sure their bodies had a language of their own with the long looks they'd exchanged and the way she felt Darien's presence without having to see her.

***

True to her word, Darien finished what she was doing and went to the barn to wash up. She didn't have to turn around to see Courtney watching her walk away, she felt her eyes boring into her. She'd been on the farm almost two months and was starting to wonder if staying had been the best idea.

Darien entered the house and took the steps two at a time. Beverly was sitting up in her bed, reading a magazine when Darien walked in.

"I hear someone's ready for another story," Darien said with a smile as she pulled the chair near.

"Actually, I wanted to thank you for helping Courtney with me," Beverly said, grabbed her hand. "I also need to apologize for my son's embarrassing behavior."

"It's okay." Darien nodded.

"That boy hasn't been the same since Boyd died. He runs around here like a rooster looking for a fight, but trust me, he's all bark and no bite." Beverly shook her head. "He thinks this farm is his and everything on it, including Courtney."

Darien furrowed her brow in question. "I don't understand. I thought he and Courtney were married."

Beverly laughed. "I think Courtney would rather till the field by hand than be married to my son." She shook her head. "No. Courtney was married to my daughter, Janice, for nearly five years before Janice passed away. They were together for about three years before that."

Darien's chest tightened in shock. She could barely breathe as she tried to force a smile on her face. The last thing she wanted to do was get involved with her donor's wife. If she'd known Janice and Courtney were married, she never would've stayed.

"Are you okay?" Beverly asked.

Darien coughed as she tried to get some air into her lungs. "Yeah…I think I inhaled some dirt in the field."

"Get a bottle of cold water out of my mini-fridge," Beverly said, pointing towards the small refrigerator.

"Thanks," Darien replied as she walked over and retrieved a bottle. She drank a long swallow, chilling her racing nerves as she peeked through the open curtains. She sighed audibly when she saw Courtney in the distance, standing in the field full of crops. "I should probably get back to work," Darien muttered as she turned away from the window.

Beverly had seen a change in Darien's demeanor when she'd told her about Courtney's marriage—her back stiffened a little straighter and her jaw clamped tight. She didn't have to guess who Darien was watching outside..

After Darien excused herself, she nearly ran down the stairs before flinging the front door wide open and taking a huge breath of fresh, country air. "What the hell am I doing?" she whispered. The last thing she wanted to do was go back out to the field near Courtney, so she went into the barn instead and began putting some of the long piping pieces together.

Chapter 15

Over the next two weeks, Darien did everything she could to avoid Courtney, but seeing her was inevitable when they were working in the same field. Courtney went through her daily routine of tending to the harvest, while Darien dug the trenches and laid the piping for the irrigation system.

The summer heat was in full bloom, scorching down on the open terrain when Courtney went inside to make Beverly's lunch. She happened to look through the kitchen window just as Darien removed her hat, pouring an entire bottle of cold water over her head. Courtney's stomach tightened in knots as the droplets of water ran down Darien's face and neck, drenching her tight, green t-shirt with Semper Fi written in large black letters over the front of it.

Beverly stood up and walked over to see what was going on since Courtney had been glued to the window for nearly five minutes, completely ignoring the burning food on the stove. She grinned when she saw Darien standing out in the hot sun in what looked like a soaked t-shirt and jeans.

"You smell something?" Beverly murmured.

"What?" Courtney mumbled. She jumped with surprise when she noticed Beverly next to her. "Shit!" she screeched when she saw the pan full of burned vegetables she was supposed to be sautéing.

Beverly laughed as Courtney ran around the kitchen, cursing and cleaning out the pan, then chopping fresh vegetables to start the meal over.

"There's no denying what's going on between the two of you." Beverly watched Courtney turn to face her. "Honey, that woman out there is already yours whether you want her to be or not."

She watched a tear roll down Courtney's cheek. "It's okay to fall in love again. That's what Janice would've wanted."

Courtney sighed and wiped the tear as Beverly stood to hug her.

"I love you like you are my own daughter. I always have and I always will. No matter who you're with."

Courtney smiled.

"If I were a little younger, I might be giving you some competition, young lady." Beverly grinned. "I've always had a thing for uniforms." She winked.

Courtney laughed and walked back to the stove.

***

Later that evening, Darien had taken a long, cold shower before lounging on the couch and listening to the radio. Her long deployments overseas and in the Middle East had trained her for a life with no TV, so she hadn't missed it at all since moving into the apartment on the farm. She was just about asleep when she heard a soft knock on the door. She got up to answer it, dressed in only a pair of black gym shorts and a white t-shirt with the Marines logo on the front.

"Is everything okay?" Darien asked, concerned to see Courtney at her door.

"Yes." Courtney smiled. "Can I come in?"

"Oh. Uh, sure." Darien shrugged and backed away.

"I need to tell you something," Courtney said nervously as she sat down on the couch.

"Alright." Darien drew in a breath and sat down next to her, not sure what she was about to hear.

"I'm not married...well not anymore," Courtney sighed. "I'm a widow." She swallowed hard when she looked up to see Darien's bright eyes looking back at her.

Darien nodded.

"I was married to Beverly's daughter, Janice." She paused. "We had a good life together. She was the love of my life...the *only* love of my life."

Darien was slightly surprised by Courtney's admission. She wasn't sure what to say to her. She felt the need to hold Courtney in her arms and run for the hills at the same time. She reached out, grabbing her hand, and looked up at Courtney with a questioning expression. The gold band was no longer on her left hand.

"I took it off." Courtney smiled softly. "It was time."

Darien rubbed her thumb over the spot where the ring had been.

"I was only twenty when Janice and I met. I was on my summer break from college and working part-time at the hardware store in town, plus part-time at the farmer's market on the weekends. I'm originally from Iowa City, but I moved to Tipton with a friend from college who was from here. I wanted a change of scenery and I honestly had no idea what I wanted to do with my life."

"What's your degree in?" Darien asked.

"Well, I was going for Political Science, but after my summer in Tipton, I never went back to school or back home to Iowa City for that matter. I fell head over heels in love with the farmer's daughter, or I guess, the farmer herself," she laughed. "We were married three years later."

Darien smiled.

"Things were great at first, but they were about as good as they could be during the next couple of years as we experienced a major drought. This farm supplies about forty percent of the inventory for the farmer's market in town, on top of being the biggest dairy farm around, so everyone was affected. It had finally started to turn around after we had one of the wettest seasons in history." She stared at the floor. "The farm was making money and everyone was happy for over a year. Then the tornado alarm sounded." Courtney wiped a tear from her cheek.

"Beverly told me. I'm so sorry," Darien murmured.

"My life drastically changed that day. Beverly was already sick and no longer working and I haven't talked to my own family in years. They sort of wrote me off after I dropped out of college. Who knows what they'd say if they knew I was a lesbian," she sighed. "Beverly is my only family, well her and Jason, so I stayed here and sort of took Janice's place, running the farm and taking care of Beverly."

"That's understandable. This is your home," Darien said.

Courtney smiled and shook her head. "Life had just about gotten back to some semblance of normal when you showed up and turned it up upside down again."

"I'm sor—"

"Don't," Courtney whispered, putting her finger to Darien's mouth. "Don't be sorry for making me feel alive again."

Darien ran the back of her knuckles over Courtney's cheek and watched her close her eyes. She leaned in, closing the short distance between them as their lips met softly.

Courtney ran her hands under Darien's shirt, feeling the ripple of her stomach muscles. Darien's chest tightened when she felt Courtney's hands on her. It had been well over a year since she'd been intimate with another woman and her body welcomed the touch.

Courtney's heart pounded. She'd never physically wanted someone so badly in her life. She was light-headed from the blood rushing to her lower extremities, but kept going, slightly praying she didn't pass out as she moved her hands higher, grazing her fingers over the bottom curve of Darien's breasts. She wanted to feel every inch of the sexy body that had been tormenting her for two months. Reaching higher, she gently messaged the firm, round breasts as she rubbed her thumbs over the erect nipples.

Darien backed away, breaking the kiss and pulling the t-shirt over her head, revealing her naked torso as she stood. Courtney swallowed the lump in her throat as she kicked off her boots and rose from the couch.

Darien wrapped her arms around Courtney's waist, kissing her hard as their bodies came together. She ran her hands beneath the tank top covering the soft, smooth skin of Courtney's back, before sliding them lower to cup the ass cheeks that had been teasing her under the cut-off shorts. With a gentle heave, she lifted Courtney easily off the ground and the smaller woman wrapped her legs around Darien's hips. She walked them over to the bed, laying Courtney down on her back as she stayed on top of her without parting their lips.

Courtney kept her legs around Darien as she ran her hands over the tight muscles of her back and up into her short hair, where she tugged playfully. Darien rocked her hips against Courtney's, causing her to gasp against Darien's mouth as their frenzied kissing continued.

Darien pulled away enough to break the kiss and look into her eyes. "We can stop," she whispered.

"Never," Courtney said breathlessly as she tried to push Darien to her back unsuccessfully.

Darien grinned and rolled over, pulling Courtney with her, who quickly sat up, straddling Darien's crotch. She rocked back and forth and bit her lower lip as she pulled her tank top over her head. Darien held her breath, watching as Courtney removed her bra, tossing it to the side with her shirt. Her eyes focused on the beautiful, perky tits and hard, pink nipples as Darien moved her hands to the slim waist in front of her, feeling the smooth skin of Courtney's body, from her tight stomach, up to the perfect breasts that were begging for attention.

Courtney put her hands over Darien's, squeezing them over her breasts and moaning while grinding against her crotch. Then, Courtney moved her hands down to the waistband of her shorts. Darien watched as she undid the button and lowered the zipper, before grabbing one of Darien's hands, pushing it down against her wet panties.

Darien locked eyes with Courtney and bit her lower lip as she sat up, pushing her fingers against the soaked fabric. The feel of their nipples grazing each other was like electricity passing between them as their lips met in another heated kiss, until Courtney pulled away and moved to the side to remove her shorts and panties.

Darien's breath caught in her throat when she took in the completely naked body of the beautiful woman in front of her. She pulled off her own shorts, adding them to the pile on the floor, before meeting Courtney's lips once again as they lie back down together, feeling all of their skin touching for the first time. Darien moved her hand between Courtney's legs, sliding her fingers through the wetness in languid circles.

Courtney panted heavier with every lazy stroke, rocking her hips back and forth and digging her short nails into Darien's back.

"Go inside," she hissed breathlessly, moaning loudly as Darien pushed two fingers deep inside of her, thrusting harder and harder.

Courtney lost control, exploding with a flash of light behind her closed eyes when her body gave way to the powerful orgasm.

Darien backed away slightly to give her some air, but Courtney rebutted the loss of contact and quickly moved closer, sliding her hand between Darien's thighs. She stroked back and forth slowly at first, while she watched the emotions play over her face.

Darien tried desperately to hold back, but it felt too damn good as Courtney's fingers rubbed her clit in a slow steady rhythm that was driving her crazy. She cried out as her body released the built up pressure with wave after pleasure-filled wave until she collapsed like a limp noodle.

Knowing they'd only broken the surface, both women caught their breath and moved together again, kissing, licking, and touching each other, climaxing over and over for the next two hours, until Courtney reluctantly pulled herself free.

Courtney couldn't leave Beverly in the house alone all night, which Darien knew and understood, but Darien still hated the cool sensation she felt over her skin when Courtney's warm body was no longer pressed against her. She kissed Courtney passionately one last time before watching her run back across the driveway into the darkness.

Chapter 16

Courtney and Darien had needed a little time to digest what had transpired between them. They'd reached pinnacles in their few hours together that neither woman had ever felt before, and they didn't know how to react. The fierce passion Courtney had experienced made her feel alive and full of desire, but it had also brought a new wave of sadness over her, knowing she'd finally moved on from her life with Janice. At the same time, Darien was overwhelmed with a mixture of emotions knowing the truth would more than likely ruin anything she had with Courtney, but also knowing she couldn't deny the fact that she was falling for her.

A few days later, a package arrived from Val. Darien headed straight to the apartment to open it, while Courtney took the rest of the mail into the main house. She still had no idea who this Valerie Sherwin person was and it bothered her.

"You've been acting different lately. What's wrong?" Beverly asked, sitting down in the home office. "Is that the mail?"

"Yes," Courtney mumbled, moving from her perch near the window to set the envelopes on the desk in front of Beverly.

Second Chance

Beverly opened everything, separating the bills from all of the other mail as Courtney walked back to the window. "You can't side step that woman forever," she chided, watching her peek through the curtains.

***

Darien tore open the large bubble envelope and dumped the contents of her California mailbox onto the coffee table. Val had tossed out all of the junk before forwarding everything else. Darien sat on the couch and sifted through the envelopes. Most of them were bill statements, which she had directly debited from her bank account. She opened a couple letters with information from her eye doctor about new organ rejection drugs that were available with less side effects, but so far, she hadn't felt anything other than an occasional bout of nausea or headache, both of which she could live with.

At the bottom of the pile was a letter from the United States Marine Corps, Department of Defense. Darien furrowed her brow, wondering what this was about, as she tore the envelope open.

SSgt. Darien K. Hollister,

This letter is to inform you that due to the successful results of your recent surgery, you may eligible to test for reinstatement of your discharge MOS/rank or general reenlistment into the USMC.

Contact MCB Camp Pendleton for further information.

Signed:
Capt. Paul J. Yarborough

Darien let go of the letter in shock. It fell to the table like a feather in the wind as she sat back. The only thing that had been on her mind since the day she opened her eyes and could see again was getting this reenlistment letter, but over the past couple of months, everything in her life had changed. Finally getting the letter after she'd all but given up on going back to the military was like a double-edged sword. No matter which side she chose, it was going to cut deep.

Just knowing that she had a chance—if only a small one, but still a chance—to put her uniform back on, made Darien sit up straight like a switch had been flipped. The military was her life. It was what she knew. Being forced to let it go had left a huge empty space inside of her. On the other hand, she'd finally learned to care for something other than the Marines for the first time in her life. She was torn between the one thing that made her whole and the only person she'd ever fallen in love with. One thing was certain, the Marines and Courtney Hollister were like oil and water and would never mix. She'd have to choose.

Darien grabbed a bottle of water from her fridge, wishing it was something stronger as she drank it down. She sat back down and penned a quick letter to Val, the only person who would understand.

Val,

I received a letter from the Captain of the Armored Vehicle Reconnaissance Company for my

Battalion Group at Camp Pendleton. I may be able to get reinstated or at least reenlist in the Marines. I only have about three weeks to decide.

Anyway, I'm letting you know that I might be coming home. Don't say anything to my parents. I will tell them when the time is right.

Darien

She hustled down the stairs and put the letter in the mailbox with the flag up before heading back out to the field to finish her work for the day.

***

Courtney sighed, watching Darien through the window as she walked back out to the field after mailing another letter, more than likely to the mysterious Valerie person. She shook the thoughts from her head and ran up to check on Beverly, who had already gone back upstairs after her meal.

"Do you need anything before I go back out?" Courtney asked, pulling Beverly's throw blanket up a little higher.

"No, I'm fine. Can you ask Darien to come to dinner? I forgot to ask her this morning."

"Sure," Courtney said flatly.

"I called and invited Jason, but he said he had other plans when I told him Darien was also invited. I wish he'd just get over the fact that he's not in control of this farm. If he keeps this behavior up, it'll never be his." Beverly shook her head.

"Get some rest. I'll be back inside in a little while to get an early start on dinner."

"Okay. Tell Darien she can come early and share another story if she wants."

Courtney nodded and walked away. She should've been happier about Darien coming to dinner, but she couldn't get past the mystery surrounding her. The fact that she'd been intimate with her only made it worse. It made her feel like she was falling for a stranger and up until that morning, she'd been slowly letting her mind picture a life with Darien.

"I only have one more section of piping to finish tomorrow, then you'll be able to plant this field," Darien said as Courtney walked closer.

"That's fine. Let Ernie know so he can start tilling as soon as it's ready," Courtney replied, as she continued past her.

Darien's mind wandered back to their night together when her eyes landed on Courtney's short, cut-off jean shorts and the expanse of tan legs under them. "Is something wrong?" she asked.

"Nope," Courtney stated without turning around. "By the way," she yelled over her shoulder. "Beverly wants you to come to dinner and she said something about a story if you finish work early."

"What about you?" Darien questioned, hurrying to catch up with her.

"Me?"

"Do you want me to come to dinner too?" Darien searched her face.

Courtney shrugged.

"I'm sorry if you feel like the other night was a mistake, but it wasn't to me. I care about you, Courtney."

"I don't know what it was." Courtney shook her head. "I don't know what we are," she snapped. "Every time I start to let my guard down, my heart tells me to run to you, but then I feel like you're a stranger. Damn it, I'm falling for you and I know nothing about you."

Darien stepped closer. "What do you want to know?"

"Why are you so secretive about your mail? You took off up to the apartment earlier like you didn't even see me standing there."

"It's just mail from home; mostly bills."

"See, I don't even know where that is. Where is your home, Darien?"

"Oceanside, California."

"Is there anyone else there? In your house, I mean?"

"No." Darien shook her head.

"What are you doing here?"

"I don't know," Darien sighed. "Something led me to you. I felt like this is where I was meant to be," she answered honestly.

Courtney saw Ernie walking towards them out of the corner of her eye and backed away to put some distance between them.

"Do you want me to leave?" Darien questioned.

"What? No. Beverly would be devastated."

"You keep talking about her, but I'm asking you. What do you want, Courtney?" Darien demanded.

"Is everything okay?" Ernie asked, causing Darien to nearly jump out of her skin. "You are the most skittish woman I've ever seen." He smiled, shaking his head.

Darien took a few breaths to slow her racing heart and calm her nerves. Her first instinct had been to fight off the enemy, and she'd nearly hit him. Darien was finding that it was easier for people to sneak up on her now that her sight was back than it had been when she was completely blind.

"We're fine." Courtney reassured him. "Just discussing a few things."

Ernie nodded. "Are you going to add in that last section of piping tomorrow?" he said to Darien.

She cleared her throat and answered. "Yeah. That was my plan. I'll have everything connected in the morning, then I'll finish burying all of the lines. You can start tilling behind me."

"That's great. I need to get those new rows of squash and okra seeds in the ground."

"It sounds like you two don't need any direction from me, so I'll leave you alone," Courtney added before walking away towards the section she was harvesting. "Dinner's at six-thirty," she called out to Darien.

"Sounds like you've been summoned." Ernie grinned. "I had my doubts at first, but you fit right in."

"Thanks." Darien looked at him through the dark lenses of her glasses "Do you think she's going to fire me?"

"Nah, that would be stupid and impulsive." He shook his head. "If there's one thing I know about Courtney Hoffman, she's very smart. That woman plans out everything she does. It drives me crazy sometimes."

Darien nodded. The Courtney she knew was quite the opposite and often unpredictable.

Chapter 17

Darien knocked on the door to the house and walked inside when Courtney answered. She was freshly showered and dressed in jeans and a white t-shirt that had the words: *First In, Last Out* written on the back of it with the Marine Corps logo in black on the front upper left chest.

"She's upstairs," Courtney mumbled, biting back the urge to kiss her.

"Can we talk later?" Darien asked, stepping closer.

Courtney nodded. She felt intoxicated by Darien's clean scent and quickly turned away before she gave in and took what her body was desperately craving.

Darien watched her walk away before taking the stairs two at a time.

Beverly was flipping the pages in a magazine when Darien popped her head through the open doorway and knocked on the wall. She smiled brightly and waved for her to come in.

"How are you?" Darien asked, removing her sunglasses.

"I have good days and not so good days."

Darien pulled the chair over to the bed. "And today?"

"It's a good one."

Darien smiled. "So, where did we leave off last time? I think I was telling you about my times as a Corporal. Is that correct?"

"I think so." Beverly smiled.

"I spent those two years doing reconnaissance training missions as a gunner and a scout as I continued earning more respect among my peers. One thing about the Marines, respect will get you everywhere. It's a brotherhood, so to speak, but there's a huge difference when a group of men respect you as a person, look up to you as their superior, and trust you with their life."

"That sounds deep," Beverly stated.

Darien laughed. "I guess it does, doesn't it?" She nodded. "I started doing everything I could do early on, so I'd keep advancing in rank when the time came. It had only taken me five years to reach Corporal, and by that point, the war on terrorism had started in the Middle East."

"How many years did you do?"

"I was coming up on my fourteenth year when I got out of the service."

"Oh, wow." Beverly grabbed her hand.

"I was promoted to Sergeant right before my first tour in Iraq where my battalion had been assigned to what was then called 'Operation Iraqi Freedom'. We were an armored assault vehicle battalion and our job was reconnaissance missions. We drove our LAVs all over the country doing area, route, and zone recon patrols, as well as low-level evacuations." Darien paused, taking a breath as she remembered the first time she killed another person.

"You just got a sad look on your face," Beverly said, squeezing the hand she was holding.

"It's funny how little things trigger the memory. Thinking back to my time in and around Baghdad and Fallujah made me remember some things—"

"Were you in heavy combat?" Beverly asked.

Darien nodded. "Off and on. We took on fire during our recon missions more times than I could ever count. I spent a year over there the first time and was promoted to Sergeant because of my impeccable record and the way I handled my leadership duties. I became a squad leader towards the end of my first tour. That promotion also made me a vehicle commander. A VC is responsible for the light armored vehicle, but also for the well being of the crew. It was a huge responsibility, but I'd earned it." Darien crossed her legs at her ankles.

"I spent a total of three years in Iraq during my four and a half years as a Sergeant. I saw various levels of combat, totaling about fifty percent of my time over there. We weren't combat patrol, but that's what we wound up doing on many occasions. You never knew what you were going to find around the next corner. Our entire battalion lost about a dozen Marines during my time there. Only two of them were with my actual company, but they'd been part of our battalion nevertheless," she sighed. She didn't need to go into the details of how many people she'd killed. She wasn't even sure of the numbers herself. It was a war zone full of bloodshed and hatred.

"Anyway," she continued. "I finally came home for good when our regiment was pulled out of Baghdad. I spent a lot of time leading training missions with my squad, as well as throughout the platoon until I went before the review board for the first time. I had an impeccable record with high marks, and all of my fitness tests scores had been some of the highest in my platoon, so when my platoon commander put in the recommendation for me to be promoted to Staff Sergeant, the board approved it. At this point, my career changed dramatically."

"How so?" Beverly asked.

"Well, as a staff sergeant, you're also the platoon sergeant, which means you're second in command for the entire platoon. You're also a section leader, which means you control two convoy squads, and you're the vehicle commander of one of those squads. Staff sergeants have a huge responsibility within their platoon. It's actually one of the hardest ranks to make in the Marine Corps, and only a small percentage of active-duty Marines can hold the rank at one time. It took me ten years to reach that level in my career. I was extremely honored."

"So, what made you get out? It seems like you loved what you were doing."

"With my new rank came a new company since you can only have one staff sergeant per platoon and all of the positions within Charlie Company were taken. I'd been moved to Alpha Company-First Platoon, which was a totally different group of Marines. I'd worked with a number of them on training missions, but I had to learn everyone's strengths and weaknesses very quickly because I was in control of the Bravo Section for the platoon, and I was also the Bravo One Squad Leader. This meant I was indirectly in charge of the fifty Marines in my platoon as the Platoon Sergeant, but I was also directly responsible for the twenty-five in my command. I know that's a lot of military jargon," she laughed.

"Basically, you were in charge? Is that right?"

"Correct." Darien nodded.

"That's impressive."

Darien smiled and continued. "I trained in my new position for about six months, running combat drills and mock recon missions. Camp Pendleton is the prime place for recon training. Anyway, not long after that, maybe a couple of months at most, my battalion was deployed to Afghanistan and assigned to Operation Enduring Freedom. Once again, I was riding all over the desert on recon missions, mapping out territory and battling insurgents with my platoon. Only this time, I was in charge of my own section, which was a convoy of two vehicles. We were basically the forward movement for the ground combat element of the war."

Darien's thoughts turned to her last weeks in the Middle East. They'd been taking on heavy fire from insurgents daily that seemed to come out of nowhere on every little turn they'd made. All of the Marines in her company were exhausted. Her platoon had been doing day and night recon patrols of different zones, on top of being sent off on special recon missions.

They'd been deployed off and on for over two years, doing two eight-month tours with only about four months at home in between. They were five months into their third tour when the attack on her convoy had happened.

Darien shook her head, trying to calm her nerves when she felt her chest tighten. She didn't know how she would ever recover from the fact that many men, women, and possibly children, were killed on her orders. And having her fellow Marines, who put their lives in her hands, also die under her command, still haunted her. She knew the convoy attack hadn't been her fault, and although the investigation proved she had known they were headed in the wrong direction, it had also shown how she honored the Marine buddy system code and chose not to break up the convoy. Those were the details that Beverly didn't need to hear. No one needed to really know the absolute hell she'd witnessed during her tours in Iraq and Afghanistan.

"Had you simply had enough of the war?" Beverly asked, breaking Darien's concentration when she saw her demeanor start to visibly change.

Darien looked up, taking a breath as she squeezed her eyes closed. "Something like that," she murmured with a nod.

"You don't have to tell me any more about the war. I can see how much it pains you. No one will ever be able to thank you enough or repay you for the service you gave this country." Beverly clinched her hand. "Leading those men and women had to have taken an act of bravery unlike any other. I think you are definitely the strongest and most courageous person that I have ever met. It's truly an honor to call you my friend."

"Thank you." Darien smiled.

"When you first arrived here, I knew you had a commanding presence and now I see where that comes from."

"There's an old saying, 'You can get out of the Marines, but you can never get the Marines out of you'. I'm pretty sure whoever said it first was right." She grinned. "Those fourteen years define me, whether I want them to or not. The things I witnessed and took part in, as well as the achievements I accomplished during that time, will stay with me for the rest of my life." She smiled softly. "Anyway, I better go see if Courtney needs a hand with dinner. I've been up here for a while."

"Oh, I'm sure it's ready by now. You go enjoy yourself. I'm feeling tired, so I think I'll rest for a while. Tell her I'll let her know if I'm hungry later."

"Okay." Darien walked out of the room, wondering if she should back out of dinner since her invite was from Beverly and not Courtney.

Chapter 18

Courtney stood at the sink washing dishes. She rushed down the stairs as soon as she'd heard Darien get up from the chair and headed directly for the sink to make herself look busy. She didn't want Darien to know she'd been standing outside the door of Beverly's room, wiping tears from her cheeks as she listened to her telling her story.

She'd learned more about Darien's life in that hour and a half than she ever could've imagined. Her private nature and noble work ethic were starting to make more sense. She stared out the window at the dusk sky as the last of the tears dried on her cheeks.

Darien was leaning against the doorjamb between the kitchen and living room when she turned around, causing Courtney to gasp loudly with surprise. She still wasn't used to Darien's eyes. Seeing the bright turquoise color across the room had also stunned her.

"How long have you been standing there?" Courtney asked, wiping her hands on a dishtowel as she glanced past her.

"Not long, maybe a minute or two." Darien shrugged. "Beverly's not coming down," she added, watching Courtney's eyes.

"Is she okay?"

"Yes. She's a little tired. She told me to tell you if she gets hungry later, she'll let you know."

Courtney nodded.

"Did you finish cooking?" Darien raised an eyebrow, looking around at the clean kitchen as she walked further inside.

"No, I haven't even started. I got busy doing other things."

Darien sighed, knowing she couldn't prolong the inevitable. "Do you want to talk about what happened earlier?" she asked, taking a seat on a stool at the corner of the island.

"It's nothing. I was just frustrated and I took it out on you. I'm sorry," Courtney murmured.

"Are you sure? It seemed like more than that."

Courtney moved closer, placing her hand on Darien's cheek. "Yes," she said smiling softly.

Darien turned on the stool, leaning into her touch. Courtney stepped between her opened legs, running her hands through Darien's short hair and across her shoulders, before leaning down to kiss her. Darien ran her hands under Courtney's shirt to the soft skin of her back, kneading the muscles up and down as she held her close.

Both women were nearly breathless as their passionate kiss ended. Courtney grabbed Darien's hands from her waist and pulled her to her feet. She raised up to her full height, which was only a few inches taller than Courtney, and immediately pulled the smaller woman into an embrace as their lips met again in another sultry kiss.

Darien saw the desire in Courtney's eyes when she stepped back, putting a little space between their heated bodies. She watched the turmoil cross Courtney's face as she looked up at the stairs towards the bedroom, then down at the floor.

"It's okay," Darien whispered, stepping closer and lifting her chin. "I'll see you in the morning." She smiled and kissed her softly, before turning and walking away.

Courtney sighed as she watched her go. She simply couldn't stomach being intimate with anyone in that bedroom—the one she had shared with her now dead wife. She had no idea how to start over with someone especially while she was also living in Janice's childhood home. No matter how long it had been since Janice died, sleeping with someone else in that bed felt wrong. But everything about the woman walking away from her had felt so damn right.

She glanced back at the stairs once more before running out after Darien. "Wait!" she yelled as she crossed the gravel driveway.

Darien spun around and smiled as Courtney jumped into her arms, kissing her with everything she had. Thunder cracked loudly and lightening lit up the night as the sky opened up with a heavy downpour. Darien set her down without breaking their arousing kiss or their carnal contact as the rain showered them. Water pelted their faces and completely soaked their clothing, but nothing seemed to penetrate the bond between their bodies.

After a very close lightning strike, they ran together towards the barn and up the stairs to the apartment. Both women were completely soaked, and the crisp air felt cool against their skin as they removed their wet clothing. Courtney noticed the tattoo on Darien's upper back between her shoulder blades. It looked like her flesh was torn open, and underneath the skin was the

Marine Corps logo with two dog tags hanging on it. Deeper into the tattoo was the symbol of a fallen soldier—a rifle in the ground between a pair of recon boots with a combat helmet on the top.

Darien turned around before Courtney could read the writing on the tags as she finished kicking off her wet jeans. Then she led Courtney to the bed where she ran her tongue over the water droplets running down her wet body.

Courtney bit her bottom lip as she leaned on her elbow, watching Darien work her way up. "Come here," she said huskily.

Darien's eyes met hers as lightning flashed across the sky, illuminating the room. She moved up, meeting her lips in a sensual kiss. Courtney wrapped her arms around Darien's back and drug her short nails across her skin as their hips met in a frenzy, rubbing back and forth.

Courtney pushed one hand down between their heated bodies, until she found the wetness she knew was waiting for her. Darien rose up slightly and mimicked her position, running her fingers through Courtney's wet folds as they lay together, trading teasing kisses and touching each other with gradual, delicate strokes.

When the noise of the pounding rain had finally subsided, it was replaced by the heavy sound of panting and breathless moaning as Courtney and Darien slowly rode the intense waves of pleasure together. They pushed away their release until they could no longer hold it back, crying out like wild animals as they finally climaxed as one.

***

Darien had no idea she'd fallen asleep when she awoke in the darkness. The sky was full of twinkling white stars, and the space next to her in the bed was cool when she ran her hand over the sheet. She lay on her back, staring at the ceiling as her mind replayed the events of entire day. She had no idea what had changed Courtney's attitude after she'd clearly been angered by something earlier in the day. Finishing the story of her time in the military had nearly torn her to pieces one layer at a time as she remembered some of the details that she'd finally forgotten, but it had made her feel like a little bit of the weight she had been carrying was lifted from her shoulders. Telling the entire story had also reminded her of how much she truly loved being a Marine.

She rolled her head to the side in the direction of the table where the letter from the Marine Corps was lying. She'd never faced a decision that she couldn't make, but she was truly torn between the Marines and Courtney. She loved them both but could only have one. Mixing the two would be impossible. She sighed and squeezed her eyes closed. Images of Courtney's naked, wet body filled her thoughts, making Darien want her all over again. That shameless desire was a need she'd never known before, and it was starting to feel really good. She tried to picture spending the rest of her life on the farm when she finally drifted back to sleep.

***

The next morning, Darien walked outside, sipping a cup of coffee as the sun was coming up over the rolling hills. She opened the tailgate of her truck and sat down.

The orange and yellow mixture of colors was breathtaking. She had seen thousands of sunrises and sunsets all over the world, and she was amazed at how they managed to look different every single time.

"It's mesmerizing, isn't it?" Courtney murmured from a few feet away.

Darien jumped with fright, silently cursing her dark peripheral vision because she hadn't seen the woman walking towards her. She grinned at the beautiful woman standing next to her and slid over, patting the open spot. Courtney smiled and sat down.

"I'm sorry for startling you. I need to remember to walk a little heavier around you," Courtney muttered.

"It's okay. I used to have ears like a dog, but my hearing seems to have failed me ever since I arrived," Darien replied as she sipped her coffee.

Courtney grabbed her free hand and squeezed it. "Do you have nightmares often?" she asked softly.

Darien stiffened.

"It's okay," Courtney murmured.

"It's gotten a little better since I've been here, actually."

"The peaceful country air is pretty soothing. I know it's helped me with painful times in my life."

Darien nodded, sipping the last of her coffee before setting the mug down next to her.

"Your tattoo is amazing, at least what I saw of it in the dim light."

"Thanks," Darien smiled.

"What is written on the dog tag?"

Darien took a deep breath, which she let out slowly before answering. "Cpl. Davidson, Cpl. Smith,

Cpl. Leonard is on one of them, and Bravo One 0313 is on the other."

"What does it mean?"

"Bravo Section, First Squad, LAV Crewman," Darien replied. "The names are the Marines that I couldn't save," she sighed as she hopped off the tailgate and headed into the barn to get the tools to start her day.

Courtney watched her walk away, knowing the pain of losing someone was hard enough. Not being able to save someone had to be the most difficult pain imaginable. She had a feeling the agony of this incredible loss and the burden of remorse were the reasons why Darien tossed and turned and awoke screaming with nightmares.

"Are you working today?" Darien smiled, stepping out of the barn with a shovel and a hoe. Her demeanor had completely changed.

Courtney grinned and pushed off the tailgate. "I need to go make Beverly's breakfast first. Would you like anything?"

"Are you on the menu?" Darien teased.

Courtney shook her head and laughed. "I'll see you in a bit."

***

"You seem to have a little more pep in your step this morning." Beverly grinned.

Courtney hadn't even noticed her when she walked inside and headed to the kitchen to open the blinds before she started preparing breakfast.

Beverly looked through the glass. "I wonder if it has anything to do with that strapping young woman who is shoveling dirt in the back field."

"I have no idea what you're talking about," Courtney replied, moving away from the window. The last thing she'd wanted to do was discuss her sex life with the mother of her deceased wife.

"Uh-huh. Well, try not to burn my omelet," Beverly teased.

Chapter 19

Later that same week, Courtney had just gotten Beverly back upstairs after her lunch when Jason's truck pulled into the driveway. She had no idea what he wanted, and she wasn't in the mood for another confrontation. Thankfully, Darien was out in the field.

"We need to talk," Jason said, walking into the house.

"Okay. What's going on?" she asked, shooing him out the front door so he wouldn't disturb his mother.

"I found this the other day," he replied, handing her an opened envelope.

Courtney realized it was a letter from the Valerie person that Darien exchanged mail with in California. "We can't read this!"

"It came to this address so we have every right. I knew she was hiding something. Go on, read it."

"Did you open this? It's against the law!"

"Oh, for fuck's sake. Whoever this Val person is, she's wants Darien to come home, and she says something about not telling this family the truth."

"What?"

"I tried to tell you and mom this woman was trouble, but neither of you would listen to me." He shook his head. "You're screwing her, aren't you?"

"Jason, my private life is none of your business!"

"I knew it!" he growled. "Read the letter and tell me letting her into your bed wasn't a mistake!"

Courtney reluctantly pulled the paper from the envelope and unfolded it.

Darien,

Ever since you came home from the war, you haven't been yourself and going to see that family was a bad idea. You've been there over three months and you still haven't told them the truth. That should tell you something. Come home and forget all about it.

I'm worried about you. Your life is here. I really think you should forget about why you're there and move on. You have your life back and that should be all that matters. I know you've always had this reckless appetite for succeeding at everything you try, but when is enough going to be enough?

And after everything you went through, do you really think going back into the service is the best thing? I know you love the Marines, but your family almost lost you. Just think about it, for me...okay? I love you and I will stand behind whatever decision you make. I won't tell your parents, like you asked, but you need to talk to them first. Whether or not you go back into the Marines, you belong in California.

We all miss you and love you!

Val

Courtney stared blankly at her hands as she folded the paper up and slid it back inside the envelope. She had a confused expression on her face when she handed it back to him.

"We need to get to the bottom of this. I want to know what she's not telling us and I want her gone!"

"Calm down. I want to know too, but there's no reason to be irrational," she sighed as she turned around and headed out to the field. Jason followed without saying anything else.

***

"Here comes trouble," Darien murmured to herself when she saw Courtney and Jason heading towards her. "Good morning," she said when they neared.

"Why are you really here?" Courtney asked.

Darien looked at her with a puzzled expression.

"You're hiding something from us and we want to know what it is," Jason added with a slightly aggressive tone.

"I'm not sure what you're talking about. I'm an employee here, doing my job," Darien replied.

"We know you're lying!" Jason yelled as he tossed the envelope at her.

Darien looked at the opened letter from her cousin and shook her head.

"Opening mail that isn't addressed to you is a federal offense," she sneered.

"Who the fuck is Val and why is she telling you not to tell us the truth? Answer me, damn it!" he shouted.

"My family is none of your concern and frankly, the contents of this letter is none of your business!" she yelled back. "So, if you don't want to go to jail, you'll get out of my face!"

"Go home, Jason!" Courtney hollered. When he looked sideways at her, she shook her head. "Just go."

Darien loosened the grip on the shovel she was holding. She hadn't even realized she'd gone into self-defense mode and was ready to run the shovel blade right through his midsection.

"Why would you lie to me?" Courtney said softly.

"I never lied to you. I don't even know what is in that letter, so how can I defend myself? I can't believe you would steal my mail and read it," she growled.

"Jason did that, but I did read it after he told me what was in it first."

"I didn't come here to hurt anyone. I went through a huge ordeal and I needed a change of scenery. It led me to you and your family," she said honestly. "I live a very private life. I thought you respected that."

"I do, but you know everything about me and my family for that matter. I know nothing about you!"

"You know a lot more than you're letting on." Darien shook her head. "I'm not stupid. I hear you run down the stairs just about every time I finish a story with Beverly. Those stories are supposed to be private."

"I—"

"I'm done talking about this. It's no one's business but my own. Now, if I'm still employed here, I have a job to do."

Courtney nodded and walked away. She had no idea what to think or even say. The woman in bed with her, the woman in the letter, and the woman standing in the field were three completely different people.

Chapter 20

The next morning, Darien had just opened the barn doors when she heard the crunch of tires on the gravel driveway. She shook her head when she stepped outside to see who it was.

"I know who you are," he growled as he climbed out. "I spent most of last night reading about Staff Sergeant Darien Hollister, the decorated war veteran." He shook his head. "Ha! Some big war hero you are. What a fucking joke."

Darien threw her arms up. "There you go," she sighed. "You know my secret."

"Oh, there's more. How are you able to see when you are blind?"

Darien balled up her fists at her sides.

"Where did you get your new eyes from? It's mighty strange how my sister dies and you show up not long after," he spat as he reached out to snatch off her sunglasses.

Darien grabbed his arm and spun him so that his arm twisted behind his back. "Don't ever try to touch me again, you pencil dick piece of shit. You have no idea who or what I am."

When she let go, Jason swung at her face, but she moved too quickly and caught him with a right hook, busting his lips.

"You crazy bitch!" he screamed as he lunged for her.

Darien anticipated his move and threw him to the ground. He got up swinging at her like a maniac, and Darien moved from defense mode to attack. Only one or two of Jason's swings connected, bloodying Darien's lip as she went toe to toe, hitting him square in the face a few times, before he tackled her to the ground.

"Knock it off!" Courtney screamed from the doorway as she ran towards them. "Stop!" she screeched at the top of her lungs.

Darien pushed Jason away from her as the gravel dust settled. She had a thin line trail of blood running down her chin and a metallic taste in her mouth, which caused her to spit a small puddle of bloody saliva on the ground. Jason's eye was starting to swell, there was blood pouring from his nose, his lip was split, and he was holding his side.

"What in the fuck is going on?" Courtney yelled.

"I'm done." Darien shook her head as she reached for her broken sunglasses. "I'm sorry, I can't give you notice, but I quit," Darien said before running up the stairs.

"What the hell happened, Jason?" Courtney asked.

"Looks like he poked a stick at the wrong bear," Beverly said from the doorway. "Come get an ice pack."

"Make her tell you," he grimaced as he walked towards the house.

Darien rushed back down the stairs and handed Courtney a piece of paper. "This is the title to the truck. Keep it, sell it, whatever. You can pick it up at the airport in Cedar Rapids."

"Don't go," Courtney murmured. "Tell me what's going on."

"I should've never come here. I'm sorry...for everything. I never meant for any of this to happen."

"Darien—"

"Tell Beverly she helped me more than she ever could've imagined and I'll never forget that." She tossed her back into the truck and turned back around.

Courtney stood a few feet away with a shocked expression on her face. Darien kissed her lips softly and whispered, "Please don't hate me. I never meant to hurt you."

Then, she got into the truck and drove away as Ernie was pulling into the driveway.

"Take the day off, Ernie," Courtney said without taking her eyes off the blue truck moving further and further in the distance. "With pay," she added.

"Did she tell you?" Jason asked, stepping up next to her with one icepack on his ribs and another on the side of his face. He watched Ernie turn around in the driveway and wave as he left.

Courtney shook her head.

"Coward," he muttered.

"What I do know is she was a Marine and she was in combat. I also know three of her people died and she tried to save them." Courtney turned and gave him the once over. "I don't think she lied about any of that."

Jason sneered.

"Care to tell me what all of this was about?" Courtney stared at him.

"She's not in the Marines anymore because her unit or convoy or whatever was attacked. A couple of the men in her command died and she was severely injured and lost her sight."

"Okay?" Courtney shrugged heavily.

"Courtney, she had an eye transplant." He watched the color drain from her face. "All of this happened around the time Janice died."

"No." She shook her head.

"It's true."

"How do you know?"

"It's all over the internet. I went to the library in town when I left here yesterday because I knew she was hiding something. She has all of these medals and a lot of the stories are about her service and the attack, but then I found a lot of articles about the transplant." He tossed one of the ice packs down and placed his cold hand on her arm. "I saw her eyes. They were brown before the surgery." He shook his head. "I'm sorry. I knew she was here for a reason."

Courtney pulled away from him as she wiped a tear from her cheek. "Don't say anything to your mom. This would devastate her," she said before walking inside the house.

"Is everything okay?" Beverly asked.

"Darien's gone."

"What has that boy done?" she shook her head.

"No, Beverly. This wasn't his fault. Not this time."

Chapter 21

Darien walked out of the airport with her suitcase in her hand. She'd changed out of her dirty, bloody clothes in Cedar Rapids before boarding her flight, so she at least looked presentable.

"Dare!" Val screeched as she ran up to her. "I can't believe you're home!"

Darien smiled and Val saw the crusted blood at the corner of her lip and scratch under her right eye.

"What happened to you?" she asked as they walked towards her car.

"Nothing. You should see the other guy." Darien grinned.

Val laughed as she drove towards Darien's house. "Are you back because you reenlisted?" she questioned cautiously.

"No. You were right. I didn't belong there." Darien shifted in her seat. "Although, I am reenlisting. I called from the airport and made an appointment for tomorrow morning."

"I can't say I understand why, because I don't, but I knew you'd find a way to get back into that uniform."

Darien nodded.

As soon as they arrived at her house, Darien tossed her suitcase on her bed and took a quick shower to wash the grime from the gravel off her body. Then, she changed into a clean t-shirt and pair of shorts from her dresser before donning her flip-flops. She searched around for a new pair of sunglasses since hers had been broken in the scuffle and finally found an old pair in a duffle bag in her closet.

"Want to go down to the beach?" Darien asked, walking out into the living room.

"You look a lot better. You need a haircut though."

Darien laughed. "Yeah, it's hard to find someone that knows how to cut high and tight in a little country town. I had to just tell them to trim it, then keep saying shorter, and shorter, until it would suffice."

Val smiled and shook her head.

"Come on, I need some sand and salt air on my skin." Darien grabbed her keys from the table and pushed the button to open her garage. "Did you drive this while I was gone?"

"Me? No. Why would I drive your motorcycle?"

"Just asking. I'm selling it anyway," she said as she opened the driver door of the car parked next to the bike, which was a silver, 1965 Ford Mustang Shelby GT350, with black rocker stripes and matching top stripes that ran the length of it.

"Why?"

"I can't see well enough to drive it." She shrugged.

"I'm sorry."

"It's okay. I still have this," Darien replied, sitting down in the driver's seat. Her knees hit against the bottom of the dash and she looked over at Val, who'd climbed into the passenger seat.

"I may have driven this one a time or two," she grinned.

"Uh-huh," Darien laughed, pushing the seat back a couple of notches.

The immaculately kept old car roared to life when she pushed the clutch in and turned the key. She put the gearshift into reverse and rolled out of the garage before pushing the button to lower the door. She sighed when her eyes caught sight of the Camp Pendleton MCB stickers in the lower left corner.

"I still can't believe you drive this thing as your regular car in this salt air."

"I didn't spend five years and a pile of money restoring it if I wasn't going to drive it. This old girl is probably more reliable than that Japanese tin-can you drive anyway," Darien retorted as she turned up the 80s hair-band tune that was playing on the radio and stepped hard on the gas pedal one time to rev up the engine. The car was built for speed, not comfort, and she loved taking it out on the highway, but they were only going down to the beach, which was about a ten minute drive out of her neighborhood and down the street.

"I didn't think you'd stay away long," Val muttered, knowing her cousin and her vices all too well. It felt good to see Darien more like her old self.

***

The next morning, Darien stepped foot on Camp Pendleton MCB for the first time since she was deployed to Afghanistan over a year ago. She was very rarely seen on the base without her uniform or some form of Marine Corps clothing on, so she'd felt almost naked walking into the office of her company headquarters in a black pantsuit and white blouse.

"Staff Sergeant Hollister?" a young man sitting at the reception desk immediately popped to attention.

"Lance Corporal," she said with a smile.

"I'm honored to see you again."

"Thank you. I have an appointment with Captain Yarborough."

"Correct. I'll let him know you're here."

She sat down and took a few deep breaths to calm her nerves.

"Look what the cat drug in," Capt. Yarborough bellowed with his deep voice.

Darien popped to attention.

"Cut the formalities. It's good to see you again, Darien," he said, holding his hand out to her.

"You too, sir."

He led her down the hall towards his office. "It's been a damn minute, hasn't it? How've you been?" he asked, closing the door behind her before taking his seat.

Darien sat down across from him. "Yes, it has. A few minutes, actually." She grinned. "I've been good. I was out in Iowa for a few months, taking in the country air."

"Oh yeah, how'd that work out for you?"

"Smells a hell of a lot better than desert sand."

He laughed loudly. "I have to say, your new eyes are definitely attention demanding. I don't think I've ever seen that color before."

"Me either, until I looked in the mirror and could see again. I scared myself quite often in the first few months." She smiled, choosing not to tell him how difficult it had actually been. She'd felt like a stranger was staring back at her and avoided looking at anything with her reflection for almost two months.

"Alright, let's get down to brass tax," he said, opening her file. "Your discharge was honorable with a medical notation. You can reenlist if the medical notation goes away."

Darien nodded.

"How's your vision?"

"It was 20/30 at my post-op."

"When was that?"

"Almost four months ago."

"Okay. Any blurred vision, double vision, or vision loss?"

"I don't have any peripheral vision at all, but other than that, everything is fine."

"The surgery alone is going to disqualify you for combat and the vision problem is going to severely limit you."

"I understand."

"You're a hell of a Marine and an exemplary leader. I'd be stupid to turn you away when you're sitting here wanting to come back after everything you've been through."

Darien nodded.

"You'll need to go through a complete medical physical and do some vision tests. Then, we can reconvene and go from there. I'll get everything scheduled. Someone will contact you with the information. Are your address and phone number still the same?"

"Yes, sir."

Darien popped to attention and shook his hand when he held it out.

On her drive home, Darien's mind raced with thoughts of going back to the life she knew so well, but the idea of doing something other than LAV Recon and Ground Combat gave her a sour taste. Since she lost her sight, she'd had to learn how to live a completely different way. The surgery helped her regain some semblance of normalcy, but she'd still had to change a few things. Going back into the Marines and picking up where she'd left off would be the one thing that could give her back the life she'd been missing. Changing her occupation specialty would just be one more thing she'd have to learn, and it'd be an ongoing reminder of what had happened to her.

Darien ran her hand through her hair. Her life had changed so much in the past year. She wondered if she'd ever find normal again. She shook her head when Courtney's image invaded her mind. Working on the Hoffman Farm had been grueling, but her time spent there was well worth it. However, letting herself fall for Courtney had been a huge mistake.

Darien maneuvered around Val's car that was parked in the driveway and pulled into the garage. Val came rushing out of the house, breaking Darien's train of thought before she could even shut off the car.

"Well?" Val asked.

"Well what?" Darien questioned with a raised eyebrow. "When did you get here?"

"A little bit ago. I hope you don't mind. I let myself in." Val grinned.

Darien smiled and nodded.

"So, how did it go? Are you back in?" Val questioned, following her inside.

She shook her head. "I have to go through some tests first."

"You don't sound very excited. Are you having second thoughts?"

"No. It's complicated." Darien removed her suit jacket and unbuttoned the cuffs of her shirt before rolling the sleeves back. "I won't be able to do the same occupation because of my peripheral vision problems. It's the only thing I know. That job is what defined me as a Marine," she sighed.

"What are they going to do? Give you a desk job?"

Darien shrugged.

"Oh, Dare." Val shook her head. "Then why go back? You retired as a decorated combat veteran. You'll never be happy doing anything else, even if you are wearing that uniform."

"I know. I'm going to go through with the tests and see where it goes. If they try to put me somewhere I don't want to be, then I won't reenlist."

"Have you told your parents?"

"No. There's no need getting them worked up if it doesn't pan out. I know they won't be happy, so I'd like to avoid that conversation as long as possible," Darien said, walking into her bedroom.

Val nodded. She didn't blame her, but she'd also been the one sitting with Darien's parents in the waiting room at Walter Reed Medical Center when the doctor told them their daughter was very lucky to be alive, but she'd also been permanently blinded by her injuries.

"Want to go get some lunch?" Darien asked, stepping back into the living room, dressed in shorts, a t-shirt, and flip-flops. "I was thinking of going to that new oyster bar down at the beach."

"Sure." Val grinned.

***

Both women were surprised at how busy the bar was. They chose a high-top table on the outside deck, overlooking the ocean. The salty breeze felt good on Darien's skin.

"I'd kill for an ice cold beer," Darien mumbled.

"Still not drinking?" Val asked, perusing the menu.

Darien shook her head. "Those therapists I saw strongly advised against drinking."

"Has it gotten any better?"

"Yes and no." Darien stared out at the water through her sunglasses. "Being in Iowa actually helped me. My donor's mother, Beverly, is an amazing lady. She's dying of Lupus, but she doesn't let it get her down."

"Aw, that's sad."

"Yeah, it nearly did me in when I found out. She was curious about my life in the service, so I'd go sit with her every couple of days and basically tell her my story. I started by telling her about my time in college. Then before I realized it, I was telling her about the Marines."

"That's interesting. How did you end it?"

"I didn't go into details about my tours during the war. I mostly told her about each of my jobs as I advanced in rank over the years. I finished with telling her I'd had enough of the war, basically."

Val nodded as the waitress came to take their order.

"Talking about my career with Beverly really helped me see past the war to the core of why I joined and why I continued to re-sign every four years. She helped me remember what it meant to be a Marine, to me anyway," Darien continued when the woman walked away.

"The therapist told you it would help if you talked. I guess you needed to find the right person to talk to."

"You know, it's odd. I never intended to tell her much of anything. It just happened. She's very good at getting people to talk."

Val smiled. "She must be because you keep a lot of shit bottled up."

Darien grinned and shook her head.

"So, you never told anyone the truth about why you were there?"

"No. I wanted to tell her, but I couldn't."

"You mentioned her daughter-in-law in one of the letters and her son. How did they take to you being there?"

"The son hated me from the start. He's a dick on a power trip because he runs the dairy side of the farm."

Val laughed. "Men are such pompous asses sometimes. What about his wife?"

Darien smiled. "Courtney isn't his wife. She was married to my donor."

"No shit?"

Darien nodded. "I didn't find out until…well, until I'd gotten to know her."

"You didn't?" Val raised her eyebrows.

"No, not at first." Darien bit her bottom lip. "She hated me too, but…things changed."

"Don't look, but the waitress at your two o'clock is checking you out."

"What?" Darien laughed.

"I'm serious. I think she's trying to get you to notice her, but little does she know she's standing in darkness," Val laughed. 'She's cute though."

Darien didn't have to turn around because the woman walked right up and offered to refill her glass, which Darien allowed.

"See, definitely flirty," Val teased.

Darien shook her head. "She's cute, but I don't need any more women in my life."

"Yeah, so this Courtney is the reason you hung around the farm, huh?" Val grinned. "Did things change in a good way?"

Darien shrugged. "I don't know. It's complicated." She'd only ever loved the Marines, and for the first time in her life, she actually loved another person. That scared the hell out of her. Jason finding out about her was the extra shove she'd needed to go back home—back to the life she knew.

"From the way you came home in a moment's notice, I'm going to assume you cut ties with everyone in Iowa and plan to never look back."

"Something like that," Darien replied as the waitress set their lunch on the table. "I'll never regret going there. It changed my life."

Val knew there was more to the story, but in true Darien form, she'd kept the details to herself. She was happy to have her home, but she had a strong feeling that Darien left a small part of her behind on that farm, just like she'd left a very large part of herself in Afghanistan—a part she'd never get back.

Chapter 22

Courtney couldn't believe her eyes when she read the information on the computer in front of her. She'd refused to believe Jason's story when he'd explained why he and Darien had been fighting in the driveway over a week ago. She couldn't let it go, so she'd driven to the local library to the Internet. Reading through the news articles had made her finally understand why Darien had left without giving her side of the story.

"Oh, my God," she whispered, reading about the attack that had blinded Darien and killed three men in her command, as well as the transplant surgery that had allowed her to see again with the help of a donor.

She looked at the dates, noting how the surgery had definitely corresponded with Janice's death. In all of their time together, she'd never known that Janice was an organ donor. In fact, she'd had no idea about the organs being removed. As her wife, it puzzled Courtney knowing that she hadn't been aware of any of this. She printed the various news reports and paid the woman at the counter before heading back to the farm. So many questions were unanswered and as much as she didn't want to hurt Beverly, she needed to know the truth—they both did.

***

Beverly had been too weak to go up and down the stairs ever since her latest setback, so she'd spent all of her time sleeping and reading the occasional magazine. The highlights of her weeks had been the days when Darien had come up to tell her some more of her story. It had only been two weeks since she'd left, but Beverly missed those hours tremendously. That was the only time she could forget for a little bit that she was battling a disease that was taking her life one day at a time.

She was just waking up from her afternoon nap when Courtney walked into her room with a handful of papers and a stern expression on her face.

"What's wrong?" Beverly asked, thinking something was wrong with one of their accounts.

"How much of her life did Darien tell you about?" Courtney asked, pulling the chair over the same way Darien had always done.

"What do you mean? She told me about her time in the service."

"Did she go into details about why she got out of the military?"

"No. Courtney, what's this about? Did you find out why she and Jason were fighting?"

"Did you know Janice was an organ donor?"

"Yes."

"When did you find out?"

Beverly sat up a little straighter. "Honey, I had no idea about a lot of things until we got to the hospital and the doctor told me."

"Where was I?" Courtney asked.

"You were sitting in a chair crying. I told him you were Janice's wife and he said I was listed as her next of kin, so he needed to inform me."

"Inform you of what?"

"That Janice was an organ donor." Beverly sat up further and patted the bed next to her. Courtney moved to her side. "She was badly injured, which you know, and the only organs they were able to transplant were—"

"Her eyes," Courtney said, cutting her off.

Beverly nodded.

"Did you know the whole time?"

"About Darien? No. The transplant information isn't given to either family from what the doctor told me. He said Janice's eyes were going to a wounded war veteran."

Courtney wiped the tears that were rolling down her cheeks.

"Darien never told me herself, but I knew the day she came to the door. I'd caught a glimpse of her eyes when she didn't think I was looking and as soon as she mentioned the military, there was no way I was letting her go."

"Is that why you asked her to tell you her story?"

"Yes. I wanted to know all about her."

"She lost her sight when her convoy was attacked. She was actually injured really badly, but she managed to pull two guys from the burning, mangled vehicle they were in together. Three other men died though," Courtney said.

"Oh, that's sad. No wonder she's so closed up. That woman has been to hell and back."

Courtney nodded. "The doctor who performed her transplant has only done a few of them, and Darien's has been the most successful so far." She shook her head. "I don't understand why she didn't tell us."

"Honey, she probably couldn't. That woman has more honor and selfless pride than anyone I've met and certainly more than most people in this world. She came here and took a hard, manual labor job for pennies because she needed to repay us for what we did for her. She knew Janice had to die in order for her to see again. I'm sure that eats away at someone like her. She didn't come here to hurt us."

"I know," Courtney sighed. "I just wish I would've known."

"Do you think it would've made you feel any differently about her?"

Courtney shrugged. "I don't know."

"You can't help who you fall in love with," Beverly said, patting her hand.

"I'm not—"

Beverly smiled. "It's written all over your face. It's the reason you've been moping around this farm for the past two weeks, and it's the reason you're wiping tears from your cheek right now."

Courtney squeezed her eyes closed. "Did you push me to go after her because you knew she had Janice's eyes?"

"No," Beverly laughed softly. "I pushed you because the way you looked at her was a way I never saw you look at my daughter." She held her hand up. "Honey, I know you loved Janice. I also know she was your first love and the love of your life. No one will ever take that away from you." She paused. "Darien is simply a different breed of woman and you're drawn to her like a moth to a flame. There's no shame in that, no matter whose eyes she's using to see."

Courtney smiled.

"You know I love you like a daughter, but I'll come back from the grave and haunt you if you don't go after her."

Courtney laughed.

"I'm serious, Courtney. Don't lose the love of your life twice. Our time here goes by too damn fast," she sighed.

Courtney nodded as she helped her lie back down. She pulled the throw blanket up and moved the chair back to the other side of the room.

"Have Cynthia stay with me. I'm sure she won't mind taking care of a sick old lady while you go get your girl." Beverly smiled softly before closing her eyes.

Courtney looked at the papers in her hand. The last page had Darien's last known phone number and home address. She looked back at Beverly before her eyes panned the room to the picture of her late wife sitting on the dresser.

"She'd want you to be happy," Beverly whispered, seeing where Courtney was looking.

Courtney looked back and smiled before leaving the room.

Chapter 23

Darien's day of testing started early in the morning in L.A. with Dr. Norton, who examined her eyes and put them through a battery of tests. From there she reported to MEPS, which is the processing station area for new recruits. There, she had a military entrance physical and blood and urine samples drawn.

Once she was finished, she went back to Oceanside to the VA clinic where her primary care doctor and regular optometrist were located. Her primary care doctor did a physical of her own plus took blood and urine samples. Dr. Feldman also looked at her eyes to give a second opinion on her vision.

Once all of the medical testing was finished, she headed over to the base for a physical fitness test that included a flexed arm hang, sit-ups, and a three mile run, all of which were timed and scored.

As soon as Darien had finished everything, she headed home to shower and relax her worn body. She'd forgotten what it was like doing a PFT. She'd never scored below a 98 in her fourteen-year career, but she'd also not physically worked out in over a year. She still ran as much as she could, and the manual labor on the farm had been more beneficial than going to a gym on most days, but she was still slightly worried. If she were going to get back into the Marines, she'd have to be perfect in every area.

It was nerve-racking having to wait for the outcome of her tests when she was used to being told her scores right away. Since Capt. Yarborough had to make the final decision, she was going to have to wait a few more days for him to call.

***

When Darien turned down her road, she noticed the back of a white, compact car parked in front of her house. She raised an eyebrow in question as she pushed the button to open her garage and pulled inside. She got out wearing her sweaty green t-shirt and shorts with MARINES written across the chest of the shirt and down the side of the shorts. She grabbed her small gym bag from the passenger seat and climbed out and shut the door.

"Nice car," Courtney said nervously as she walked up the driveway. She was uneasy about seeing Darien again, but all of her apprehension was gone as soon as she laid eyes on her.

Darien dropped the bag. "Courtney?" she gasped, resisting the urge to pull the smaller woman into her arms.

"Hi," Courtney murmured.

"What are you doing here?"

"Can we talk? I just want the truth…from you. I need to know."

Darien nodded and motioned for Courtney to follow her inside of the house.

Courtney looked around when she crossed the threshold. Darien's house was decorated like a beach house in whitewashed wood and various shades of blue. The floor plan was open with living room, dining room, and kitchen combining to make up one half of the house. The other side of the house had a large master bedroom and two small guest rooms, one of which doubled as an office with a desk and a bookcase full of books. There was a small, covered deck off the back of the house where a grill and a small table set was located.

"Do you mind if I shower?" Darien asked.

Courtney had noticed she was in sweaty gym clothes. "What were you doing before you came home?"

"I've been doing medical and fitness testing for the Marine Corps all day."

"So, you're going back in then?"

Darien shrugged. "Maybe. If I pass all of their tests. I'll be out in a minute. Make yourself at home," she said as she walked into her bedroom. "There's not a lot of food in there. Val and I have been going out to eat all week," she called from the other room.

Courtney couldn't stand it anymore. She got out and stormed into the bedroom, but Darien was already in the glass shower. She could see a distorted image of her under the spray. Courtney snatched the door open, causing Darien to shriek.

"Who is this Val person? Is she your girlfriend? Wife?" she growled. "I need to know if some woman is going to come home and throw me out on my ass."

Darien shook her head as she squirted soap into her hand and began lathering her upper body. "Val? Val's my cousin. She's my lifeline—my best friend. I don't know where I'd be or what I'd be doing without her. She lives about 45 minutes away in San Diego, where she owns a consulting firm. She might call while I'm here, but she's not going to show up. She has meetings up in Los Angeles all week." Darien stepped under the spray to rinse the soap. "Now, if you'll excuse me, I'll be out in a few minutes."

Courtney stared at the beautiful turquoise eyes looking back at her. *Janice's eyes.* She thought as she nodded and shut the door. She'd tried to forget what Darien's naked body had looked like and seeing her again brought all of the desire back to the surface. She walked out of the bedroom, towards the kitchen, looking for something to take her mind off the naked, wet woman in the other room. She'd never wanted to take a shower so bad in her life.

As soon as Courtney sat down on the couch with some mail catalog she found on the kitchen counter, Darien appeared in the doorway, dressed in a t-shirt and shorts.

"I'm sorry," Courtney muttered.

"It's fine. I should've told you about her a long time ago. Hell," she said, sitting down next to her. "I should've told you about a lot of things."

Courtney nodded.

"Jason probably said a lot after I left."

"Yeah, that's an understatement. I thought he was nuts until I went and read the articles myself." Courtney reached out, grabbing Darien's hand. "Were you really blind?"

Darien pursed her lips and nodded.

"And now?"

"I don't have any peripheral vision on the sides, it's completely black, but my central vision is fine."

"Those men that died in your convoy…are they the names on the dog tags in your tattoo?"

"Yes," Darien said softly.

"What made you come to Iowa? To our farm in particular?"

"You know why," Darien sighed. "Look at my eyes."

Courtney reached up, rubbing her hand along the side of her face. "I had no idea. Beverly knew as soon as you'd arrived, but that's because she'd known about the transplant. I was beside myself with grief and that's why she never told me. I thought it was a pretty strong coincidence that you both had the same color eyes, but that was all it was, at least until Jason said you'd been blinded in the war and had an experimental eye transplant surgery right around the same time that Janice died."

Darien nodded. "I hate that she had to die for me to be able to see again. I'm sorry."

"It's not your fault. I'm glad she was able to help you. If she'd had a choice, she would've done it to help you. That's the kind of person she was. It's also why she was an organ donor, which was another thing I never knew about."

"I should've never gone to see your family, but after sitting here for three months, the guilt had started eating me away. It tore me apart knowing someone had to die in order for me to see again. I went there thinking I'd tell my donor's family who I was and thank them for the gift that I'd received, but I froze when I arrived. Ernie saw me and immediately thought I was looking for work. He introduced me to Beverly and after meeting her, I knew she was Janice's mother. She told me she was ill and didn't get around much, which was why they were looking for help."

Darien stared down at the floor. "I felt like it was my duty to help her, so I took the job. I was only going to help get the repairs caught up. I never planned on staying."

"Why did you stay?"

"You." Darien looked at her. "I didn't know who you were until it was too late. I thought you were Jason's wife. Beverly mentioned her son and daughter-in-law." She shook her head. "I kept thinking, why is she with this asshole? Then when you said you weren't with him, I let myself fall for you. I never imagined you were Janice's wife."

"I'd never been with anyone until I met her. When she died, I thought I'd never be with anyone again. We live in such a rural area. For two lesbians to find each other there was damn near a miracle. So I thought finding love again would be nearly impossible. At least it was until you appeared on our property."

"If I'd known from the beginning, I never would've—"

"Yes," Courtney said, cutting her off. "We both would have because you can't help who you fall for, no matter how hard you try to fight it."

Darien squeezed the hand holding hers. "Where does this leave us?"

Courtney shrugged. "You're going back to the Marines and I have to be back at the farm tomorrow."

"Who is with Beverly? I thought about that while I was in the shower, but you scared that thought away when you opened the door."

Courtney smiled. "Ernie and his wife are with her."

Darien nodded. "Does this mean you're spending the night?"

Courtney shrugged. "Well, here or a hotel. I was hoping you'd show me what your life is really like because this is about as far away from a farm as you can get." She grinned.

"Come on." Darien winked and stood up with her hand out to Courtney.

"I should've known you were into old cars when you pulled up at the house in that truck," Courtney said, sliding into the front seat of the Mustang.

"I've always loved classic cars and speed. I actually restored a lot of this one myself. It took five years start to finish," she said, starting the car and backing out of the garage.

"I see your love for music followed you to the farm too," Courtney said over the blaring radio that came on as soon as the car was started.

"Yeah, sorry," Darien laughed, turning the music down as she drove down the road. "Do you like seafood?"

"Yes, although we only get the frozen kind where we live."

"There's a really great oyster bar down here on the beach. We can have lunch and maybe take a walk."

"Sounds good," Courtney replied, looking around as they drove through the back of Darien's neighborhood towards the beach.

***

Courtney couldn't believe the view of the ocean as she ate her lunch. She'd only seen the beach in pictures and on TV, but neither of those compared to being there in the flesh.

"It's beautiful here. I can see why you call this home." Courtney smiled.

"Yeah, I've spent a lot of time on this beach over the years."

"Back again so soon?" The waitress who had flirted with Darien the last time she was at the restaurant came over with a pitcher of iced water. "Can I get you a refill?"

Darien smiled and slid her glass over so she could top it off. The young woman winked at her before walking away.

"Who is that?" Courtney asked with a raised eyebrow.

Darien shrugged. "Val and I had lunch here a couple of weeks ago. I guess she remembered me."

"Uh huh."

Darien tilted her head to the side. "Are you jealous?" she asked as she paid the check. "Actually, she probably thinks I get around since I was just here with another girl recently."

"Why would I be jealous? You have your own life and a lot of people in it apparently."

"My last steady girlfriend was when I was in college," Darien murmured. "No one seemed to want to hang around long enough for me to come home from deployment, so I gave up after a while. I don't have a revolving door on my house or anything like that, but I've had a few companions over the years."

Courtney grabbed Darien's hand, lacing their fingers together as she eyed the waitress on their way out. Darien led them down the path to the thick sand.

"I can't see you being alone long. You're an amazing person that most people should admire, and you're as hot as fire on a cold winter day," Courtney said, running her thumb over the back of Darien's hand as they walked.

Darien smiled and walked them down to the water.

"I've never been in the ocean!" Courtney squealed as the water lapped against her ankles.

"Well, now you can tell everyone you stepped foot in the Pacific Ocean!" Darien exclaimed, reaching down to splash her a little bit.

"Stop!" Courtney shrieked, quickly letting let go of her hand as she ran away from the water before Darien could soak her.

"Alright," Darien laughed, catching up to her.

They walked a little further down the beach, away from the tourist shops and restaurants to a more private area for locals. Darien walked up to a spot and sat down. Courtney joined her.

"When I recovered from my injuries enough to come home, Val moved in to basically take care of me. She was able to run her business remotely, which helped me out tremendously. I spent countless hours sitting right here, feeling the heat on my skin, listening to the waves crash against the shore, and staring at nothing but darkness. Those were the longest and most difficult three months of my life."

Courtney ran her hand up and down Darien's back outside of her t-shirt.

"I thought my life was over, and in way, it was. The life I knew died inside of that burning wreckage, along with three young men who had their whole lives ahead of them."

"I read the news stories," Courtney murmured.

Darien shook her head and sighed. "That's exactly what they are...stories. The media never did get the whole truth and they never will. Some things are better left unsaid." Darien turned her head so she could see the woman sitting next to her. "Anyway," she continued. "After sitting here for three months, mourning the life I had and the men I'd lost, my eye doctor introduced me to an ophthalmologist who had been working on experimental eye transplant surgery. I met with him, agreed to do the procedure, and well...you know the rest."

"Did you come back here once you could see again?" Courtney asked.

Darien stared out at the ocean. "Yes. I came right back to this very spot where I'd sat before. It was bittersweet being able to see this view once again, knowing someone had to give their life in order for it to happen." She turned towards Courtney. "The next three months ate me up. I couldn't think of anything except saying thank you to my donor's family. Val thought I was nuts when I booked a flight and took off on a whim."

"I'm glad we got to know you." Courtney smiled. "You know, Beverly asked me if I thought things between us would've been different if I'd known why you were there from the beginning."

"What did you to tell her?"

"I said I didn't know. But she knew better than that and called me out on it," she said, moving closer as Darien wrapped her arm around her.

"How can two totally different lives meet in the middle?" Darien sighed.

"They can't," Courtney murmured.

***

The next morning, Courtney peeled herself out of Darien's arms at the airport and boarded the plane with tears in her eyes. She knew she was walking away from her second chance at love, but she'd made a promise to Janice that if anything ever happened to her, she'd take care of Beverly. Which was the only reason she was able to get on that plane without looking back.

Darien didn't have a ticket, so she couldn't go any further than the security checkpoint. As soon as they'd said goodbye, she went outside and waited for Courtney's plane to take off. She knew the airline and the departure time, so she was pretty sure she could figure out which one she was on. A tear rolled down her cheek as the Delta plane flew overhead just after nine o'clock. As soon as the white plane was out of sight, Darien walked to her car and headed home. She knew Courtney needed to take care of Beverly and run the farm. She also knew that life on the farm would never be enough for her.

Chapter 24

A week went by before Darien was called to meet with Cpt. Yarborough about the results of her testing. She was slightly nervous as she dressed in a white blouse and charcoal gray pantsuit. She felt butterflies in her stomach, making her want to puke in the passenger seat of her car as she headed to the base.

When she arrived, she took a deep breath and smacked her cheeks a few times to try and calm her nerves. She couldn't believe how she could participate and command recon missions in the middle of war with insurgents trying to kill her at every flank and have no issues with her nerves. Yet, here she was awaiting simple test results and she couldn't seem to keep her hands from shaking and her stomach from rolling.

As soon as she finally gathered the courage to walk into the building, she was shown to the captain's office where he was awaiting her arrival.

"I have great news, good news, and other news," he said, shaking her hand. "Have a seat."

Darien sat down across from him and held her breath.

"I've known you for a long time, and I was proud to serve next to you in peace time and in combat. You were a damn good Marine and a hell of a section leader."

He opened the file in front of him and sighed. "Your FIT test was outstanding as usual. Your MEPS physical and post surgery exams are both fine. Based on all of those results, you can reenlist as early as tomorrow, but not having peripheral side vision completely disqualifies you from infantry. You will have to change your MOS." He watched the color drain from her face. "I'm sorry, Darien. I know how much you loved your job."

Darien nodded. She wasn't quite sure what to say.

"You can crossover at your same rank to either administration, logistics, supply, communications, retention, or training. Any of those MOSs I just listed would keep you at the same rank/rate of pay. You would need little to no training, depending on which one you chose."

Darien swallowed the lump in her throat.

"Now, knowing you personally, I think retention could be good. You could always rotate out of that after a while, or training. You're one of the best section leaders I've ever seen. You'd make one hell of a drill instructor. I don't know how connected you are here in California, but you'd have to transfer to Parris Island and move across the country. You could also stay here with the Camp Pendleton School of Infantry as a marksmanship instructor, but I personally think combat instructor has your name written all over it. If you can't be part of an LAV battalion anymore, why not train those want to be in your shoes as LAV Crewman and officers of LAV platoons? You know that job inside and out and you can do it right here."

Darien nodded.

"You already have fourteen years in and have had a very rewarding career, but if you sign on for another six, you will probably retire at E7 or E8, which is an outstanding career for an enlisted Marine. That's something to think about as well. Go out on your own terms and at the top of your game."

"You've definitely given me a lot to think about," she said honestly. "Do you mind if I take a few days to mull this over?"

"No. This is your life and your career. You decide what's best for you."

"Thank you, sir."

She walked out of his office with a blank look on her face. She'd never felt such extreme highs and lows in a matter of fifteen minutes. She felt like she was going to puke as she started her car and drove away.

***

Darien spent the next two days walking along the sand and listening to the waves while she tried to decide what to do with her life. It made her think of Courtney. She wondered what she'd say about the decision. She knew Val would tell her not to start over, so she hadn't bothered calling her. Darien's family was completely against her going back into the service at all. Even though she'd never be in combat again, they were happy to have her home, living the civilian life.

She hadn't done much financially in the last fourteen years except purchase her house and restore her Mustang, but being out of work for a year was starting to impact her savings account. She needed to go back to work at some point. There was nothing she'd rather do than wear that uniform again and she knew it, but there was absolutely no way she was taking a desk job. Moving across the country was out of the question as well.

She smiled, thinking Capt. Yarborough had known her all too well and had probably already started the paperwork for her to reenlist with the new MOS as a Combat Instructor. She picked up a small rock and tossed it out into the ocean as far as she could.

Darien was feeling the weight lifting from her shoulders. She'd made her decision, which had actually taken very little effort once she really thought about what mattered most to her. If she couldn't be on the frontlines, leading a recon mission and doing what she loved, then she'd do her damndest to train the Marines who would fill her shoes.

She sat down in the thick sand, pulled her phone from her pocket, and called the number in her contacts for Capt. Yarborough's office.

***

As soon as she'd hung up with the captain, she called Val to give her the good news, which Val wasn't too happy about, but she'd told her she loved her and stood behind her decision.

Then she made the call to her parents that she'd been dreading. Her mother cried, but she felt a little better knowing that Darien would be safe because she'd never physically be anywhere near another war. Both her parents and Val had asked for the reenlistment date so they could be there to witness her being sworn in again. She'd told them it was set for Wednesday of the following week. She'd also said there would probably be media there. News of her return to the Marine Corps was a big deal. After everything she'd gone through in the last year, the Marine Corps wanted people to know how honored they were to have her back and to showcase the incredible amount of heart and dedication Darien had for her country.

Finished with all of her conversations, Darien locked the screen on her phone and leaned back on her elbow to watch the sunset. In less than a week's time, she'd no longer be a retired veteran. The sound of active duty Marine sounded a hell of a lot better.

Chapter 25

Beverly watched Courtney move around her bed, straightening the blankets after giving her a much needed sponge bath. She'd had another setback and barely had the strength to sit up. Courtney had purchased a beside toilet a few days earlier, allowing for easier access since she could barely walk a few steps without getting too winded to breathe.

She'd noticed a difference in her demeanor since she'd come back from California. They hadn't talked much about the impromptu trip, but there was no denying the sadness in her eyes.

"You miss her, don't you?" Beverly murmured breathlessly.

"What was that?" Courtney asked, sitting down on the edge of the bed. "Do you need me to freshen your drink?"

"No." Beverly cleared her throat, trying to catch her breath. "I said you miss her. I can see it all over your face."

Courtney shrugged. "You can't miss something you never really had to begin with." She patted Beverly's hand. "Darien's life is in California—in a Marine uniform. Mine's here on this farm—with you. Nothing

166

will ever change that." She stood up. "Get some rest. I'll make you some soup in a little bit."

"Courtney," Beverly said with a raspy voice.

She spun around and walked back over to the edge of the bed. "Do you need anything else?" Courtney asked softly.

"When I'm…gone…live your life."

Courtney smiled and patted her hand.

"This was always…Janice's life," she gasped. "If you love Darien…run to her…and live…Courtney's life."

Courtney wiped the tears from her cheek.

"Promise…me," Beverly rasped.

Courtney nodded and bent down, kissing her cheek. "I promise," she whispered.

Then, she walked out of the room before the waterfall of tears began rushing down her face. Losing Janice was the hardest thing she'd ever dealt with, and Beverly had been there to help her through that. Now, she was losing Beverly, and the only person she wanted comfort from was on the other side of the country. The only thing she'd known since was twenty years old was that farm and Beverly was right. It had been Janice's life, but it was also hers.

Chapter 26

On Tuesday, Darien had her hair cut early. Later that afternoon, she picked up the pants and jacket of her Dress Blue uniform from the dry cleaners, where she'd had it cleaned and pressed. The last time she'd worn it, she was being awarded the Silver Star and Purple Heart in front of her entire battalion.

She hung the midnight blue colored jacket with red trim on the back of the bathroom door. Then, she meticulously pinned her ribbon board over the left chest, along with her Rifle Expert Badge, which she placed under the board. She added the gold Marine Corps, Eagle Globe Anchor insignia to both sides of the standing collar. Then, she took the sky blue pants with the red, non-commissioned officer stripe down the sides and hung them both in the front of her closet door. Finally, she removed her stark, white cover from its protective box and placed it on the nearby shelf, next to her pristinely polished black shoes.

In less than twenty-four hours, she'd be on active duty again. She was nervous and excited at the same time. She looked at her uniform one last time, feeling pride course through her veins.

After closing the closet door, she walked across the house to the kitchen. She noticed the blue light blinking in the corner of her phone, indicating she had a missed call. She swiped her finger over the screen and Ernie's name came up. He hadn't left a voicemail, so she quickly called him as she sat down on the couch.

"Hello?" he answered after a couple of rings.

"Ernie? It's Darien Hollister. Did you call me?"

The phone was silent for a minute.

"Are you there?" she asked.

"Yes. Sorry, I needed to walk outside." He cleared his throat. "I was calling to tell you that Beverly passed away last night."

"Oh, my God," Darien gasped.

"She went peacefully," he added. "Jason is beside himself, so Courtney made all of the arrangements. She's trying to be strong, but I know this is difficult for her."

Darien felt so bad for Courtney and the only thing she could think of was holding her. "When is the funeral?" she questioned.

"It's tomorrow at 11:30a.m."

Darien grabbed a pen and a piece of paper. "What's the name of the cemetery?"

"It's not at the cemetery. She's being cremated today and there will be a memorial service tomorrow on the farm where her ashes will be scattered. This is the same thing they did when Janice died."

"Okay."

Darien finally let the tears flow from her eyes when she ended the call. So much had changed in her life because of Beverly and her family. She wanted nothing more than to be there with them. She picked up the phone and called Capt. Yarborough's office and left a message with his assistant that she'd had a death in the family and had to travel out of state immediately, so she needed to move her swear-in date back. Capt. Yarborough called her back a few minutes later to give her his condolences and let her know they'd moved the date back to the following Monday, but couldn't push it any further because she needed to go through a two-week training process before the new recruits came in. Darien completely understood and told him she would be there, along with her family.

She quickly got online to research flights. The only one that would get her there on time flew out of San Diego later that evening and arrived in Cedar Rapids at nine the next morning, after a two and a half hour layover in Chicago. Darien quickly booked the flight and a rental car from the airport.

After that, she called Val and her parents to let them know that the swear-in ceremony had been pushed back to Monday. They were all sorry to hear about Beverly's passing, and her parents said they'd change their flight. Darien told them to change it to Thursday and Val would drive them up to Oceanside since they were flying into San Diego. That way, they could spend the whole weekend together, which was something they hadn't done in a long time.

***

Later that evening, Darien looked at the uniform that was hanging in her closet, awaiting one of the biggest days of her life. Knowing there was no better way to honor Beverly and their time together, she began removing the jacket and pants from their hangers. Since she was flying all night and going straight to the service, she wouldn't have time to stop and change clothes, so she had to fly in her uniform—something she'd never done before.

When she'd finally finished dressing, Darien turned around and looked in the mirror, gasping when she saw herself again for the first time in over a year. Tears rolled down her cheeks. She was overcome with grief for the tragedy that took her sight along with three men's lives. She also felt heavily honored for the privilege to be able to wear that uniform once again. She stood up straight and wiped away the tears.

***

The hustle and bustle of the airport was almost nonexistent at nine o'clock at night as Darien walked through the security checkpoint. She showed her military ID and was escorted around the scanning machines since the metal on her uniform would cause the detectors to go off. She noticed a few stares as she made her way down to the course where her gate was located. The plane was scheduled to take off in less than an hour, so she sat down away from the crowd of people who were also getting onto her flight.

The woman closest to her had tried to make small talk, but when Darien informed her that she was on her way to a funeral, the woman politely gave her condolences and went back to the book she was reading.

When the initial boarding call began, everyone at the gate stood up and turned their attention to Darien. A flight attendant taking the same flight stepped over to her.

"They're waiting for you to board first," she whispered.

"Why is that?" Darien asked.

"Respect." She smiled.

Darien nodded and stood up straight as she walked past everyone. She crossed the threshold onto the plane and checked her ticket for the coach class seat number.

"Ma'am," the captain held his hand out. "It's a pleasure to be your pilot this evening."

"Thank you," she murmured.

"Your seat is this way," the flight attendant next to him said, waving her hand towards first class.

"My seat is number 23A," Darien said to her.

"A first class passenger offered his seat to you."

"Okay." Darien nodded, slightly confused. She'd never been on a civilian airline while in uniform, so she was taken aback at the preferential treatment from this stranger. When she'd travelled back and forth from the Middle East to California on leave, she'd always flown on a military transport plane. "Please tell him I said thank you," she murmured, sitting down in her new seat. She looked out the window at the tarmac, thinking about the reason she was on the plane in the first place and wiping a single tear from her cheek.

Chapter 27

Courtney sat in the front row of the gathering, with Jason next to her, holding her hand. Directly across from them was a small stand with a silver urn sitting in the middle and a large picture of Beverly next to it. Behind them were two more short rows of chairs, which were filled with Ernie and his wife, as well as employees from the dairy side of the farm and various other people who knew the family.

Darien arrived with a minute to spare and walked up with the last of the people who took their seats. She stood at attention behind the last row as the reverend began his speech. As he talked, she thought about Cpl. Davidson, Cpl. Leonard, and Cpl. Smith, the three men she'd lost. She was still in the hospital, recovering from her injuries when they'd all had their funerals. One of the first things she'd done when she got her sight back was visit their memorial sight on the base. They'd all been buried in Arlington National Cemetery, and she swore she'd go visit soon to pay her respects.

When the reverend ended his eulogy and said a prayer, he asked the family members to speak. Jason was too distraught, so he shook his head no, but Courtney stood and walked up next to him. She kissed her fingers, then placed them on the urn before turning around to face

173

the small crowd of ten or so people. Her eyes immediately fixed on the person standing in the back, in the immaculate uniform. It was no doubt the only person she'd been wishing to see in the last twenty-four hours. She wiped away tears with a wadded up tissue as she spoke.

"Beverly was not only my mother-in-law, she was basically my mother too. She took me into her family with open arms, taught me a lot about love and about life. If she cared for you, you knew it because she never held anything back. We went through the hardest loss in our lives together when my wife Janice passed away tragically. I think that caused us to grow a bond like no other." She sniffled, wiping more tears.

"When Beverly first got sick, I promised Janice that I'd be there for her if anything ever happened to her or Jason and I kept that promise, but it wasn't a promise to me, it was privilege and a honor to be her caretaker. I loved her like she was my own mother."

Courtney looked at the uniformed woman and smiled. "Over the past six months or so, a stranger came into our lives and made the two of us almost whole again without even realizing it." She paused. "You held a very special place in Beverly's heart and she told me when I saw you again, to tell you she loved you," she said directly to Darien.

Darien nodded slightly, but kept her stance at attention.

Courtney turned to the urn and put her hand on it again.

"I love you, sweet woman. I know you're up there right now with Janice, looking down." She kissed her fingers and placed them on the urn once again.

Then, she walked up and grabbed Jason's hand, tugging softly as he rose from his chair. Courtney held his hand as she picked up the urn.

"If you will all rise, the family would like to walk down the hill a little ways to let the ashes go in the wind, scattering over the fields and rolling hills of the property," the reverend said.

Darien stayed in the back as the small group followed Jason and Courtney. When they reached the chosen spot, Jason kissed the side of the urn.

"I love you, mom. I promise to do you proud," he whimpered.

Then, he and Courtney removed the lid and shook the ashes up into the air. The breeze carried the powdery substance off like a cloud of dust, before it disappeared. Jason placed the lid back on and turned around to receive the people who were waiting to give their condolences. Courtney sidestepped and rushed around everyone.

Jason and Ernie watched as she jumped into the arms of the woman in the Marine Corps. uniform. Ernie smiled and Jason shook his head. He had nothing but respect for her after Courtney returned from California and explained Darien's true story to him and Beverly.

***

Darien wrapped her arms around Courtney, lifting her off the ground in a tight embrace that felt better than the uniform ever had. She was reluctant to let her go, but she set Courtney back on her feet anyway.

"I didn't know how to tell you," Courtney said softly. "I kept thinking about you and how much I wanted you here. Then, I looked up and there you were, just the way Beverly would've wanted to see you. She admired and honored you so much. You were a hero to her."

"She had no idea, but she was my hero. It's because of her that I had the mental strength and courage to go back to being a Marine. She helped me see past the PTSD and the war, to the loyalty, honor, respect, and brotherhood that were the reasons I became a Marine in the first place."

Courtney stepped back, looking her up and down as she shook her head.

"What?" Darien asked.

"You look so different." She smiled. "This definitely looks better on you than jeans and work boots, although that looked pretty good too!"

Darien laughed.

"So, it's official then, you're back in the service?" Courtney said as she watched the people starting to make their way up to the house.

"I've signed all of the papers, the only thing left is to be sworn in."

"When is that?"

Darien smiled. "Right now."

"Oh, no."

"It's okay. They moved it to Monday so that I could be here."

"Are you able to stay for a day or two?"

"No. My parents are flying in tomorrow, so I need to catch a return flight this afternoon."

Courtney nodded, lacing their fingers together as they walked along the property.

"What are you going to do now? With the farm, I mean," Darien questioned.

Courtney sighed. "I don't know. All of this," she waved her arms out. "Belongs to Jason now. I own Janice's portion, but he has the majority because I'm sure Beverly left him her portion."

Darien stopped walking and pulled Courtney into her arms.

"Come home with me," she said without thinking, which was something she never did.

"What?"

"I'm serious. Janice and Beverly are gone. There's nothing holding you here anymore. You said it yourself—this farm is Jason's. Live the next act of your life with me, in California."

Courtney shook her head. "I'd still be alone. You deploy all over the world, and no matter what the government says, we're still at war. I couldn't bare losing you, too."

"You won't lose me." Darien sighed. "I can't get deployed. I'm not part of infantry anymore because of my vision. I'm going to be a combat instructor at the School of Infantry on the same base where I was stationed."

Courtney blew out a heavy breath.

"I promise not to leave you," Darien murmured as she bent her head, kissing her softly.

Courtney closed her eyes and leaned into her, deepening the kiss, before pulling away.

She shook her head. "You can't promise me that. Everything I love leaves me," she cried. Wiping the tears from her face, she continued, "It's better for me to say goodbye now, than to start a life with you. I'm sorry."

"Then, I won't go back. I'll stay here with you. I did the farm thing once. I can do it again. Hell, we could get our own farm, if that's what you want," Darien had no idea what she was saying. All she knew was she was madly in love for the first time in her life and it hurt too much to be away from Courtney.

"You'd do that? For me?"

"I'd do anything for you," Darien relied.

"Look at you. You're not a farmer." Courtney smiled. "You're a Staff Sergeant in the United States Marine Corps. That's not only what you are, it's who you are."

Darien nodded, knowing she was right.

"You know, not long before she passed, Beverly told me to live my life. I'm not exactly sure what that is anymore, but you...you know exactly what your life is, Darien. Go live it. This is your second chance."

Darien hugged her and kissed her lips softly. "It's your second chance too," she said softly, looking into her eyes one last time before walking away.

Courtney knew she was right. That's what Beverly had meant all along, but she was scared to start over. She went back to the house and up to her room, where she ignored the funeral guests and cried herself to sleep.

Epilogue

Darien stood at attention in front of Capt. Yarborough, her parents, Val, and a few other Marines, whom she'd chosen to witness her being sworn in. She raised her right hand and began the oath.

"I, Darien Kathryn Hollister, do solemnly swear that I will support and defend the Constitution of the United States against all enemies, foreign and domestic; that I will bear true faith and allegiance to the same; and that I will obey the orders of the President of the United States and the orders of the officers appointed over me, according to regulations and the Uniform Code of Military Justice. So help me God."

"Welcome back to the Marines, Staff Sergeant Hollister," he said proudly as he saluted her.

Darien returned the salute, then smiled and turned to her family with tears in her eyes. She cocked her head to the side when she noticed someone standing in the back of the room behind her parents.

She heard a loud "Ohh rah!" from a couple of men whom she served in the war with and had asked to be witnesses. She turned and smiled at them as they picked her up onto their shoulders in celebration of her reenlistment.

"Okay, okay. Put me down," she laughed.

Capt. Yarborough shook his head and smiled. "Go be with your family," he said. "Report to your knew MOS at 0800 tomorrow."

"Yes, sir," she popped to attention with the other enlisted Marines in the room as he walked out.

"I'm so proud of you," Val squealed, hugging her.

Darien moved from her cousin to her parents and that's when she saw Courtney standing a few feet away, smiling brightly at her.

"Oh, my God! What are you doing here?" Darien ran over, picking her up off the ground in a loving embrace that caused the room to go silent. She quickly set her down and grinned sheepishly.

"I let you walk away from me twice, Darien Hollister, and I'm never doing that again." Courtney put her hand on Darien's cheek. "I love you and can't imagine my life without you in it." She smiled. "I'm sorry it took me so long to realize that you and Beverly were both right. That farm isn't my life anymore, you are."

Darien shook her head and smiled. "I love you too—more than I've ever thought I could love someone," she replied, kissing her softly.

The other Marines hooted and hollered, causing them to both laugh.

"Mom, Dad, and Val, this is the love of my life, Courtney Hoffman," Darien said, stepping back to let them all get acquainted.

As Darien stood there in her dress blue uniform with her fellow Marines, she felt whole again. But, looking at her family that now included Courtney, she felt complete. She squeezed her eyes closed, remembering for a brief second what the darkness had felt like, before opening her eyes and silently thanking the powers-that-be for her second chance.

About the Author

Sydney enjoys reading everything from magazines to historical books and boasts about her massive collection of paperbacks and hardbacks in her personal library. She's also a huge fan of multiple TV shows, which she says take up too much of her time. She enjoys writing novellas and is the author of the bestselling novellas: *One Night* and *Shadow's Eyes*. *Second Chance* is her first full length novel.

Other Titles Available From
Triplicity Publishing

Meant to Be by Graysen Morgen. Brandt is about to walk down the aisle with her girlfriend, when an unexpected chain of events turns her world upside down, causing her to question the last three years of her life. A chance encounter sparks a mix of rage and excitement that she has never felt before. Summer is living life and following her dreams, all the while, harboring a huge secret that could ruin her career. She believes that some things are better kept in the dark, until she has her third run-in with a woman she had hoped to never see again, and gives into temptation. Brandt and Summer start believing everything happens for a reason as they learn the true meaning of *meant to be*.

Coming Home by Graysen Morgen. After tragedy derails TJ Abernathy's life, she packs up her three year old son and heads back to Pennsylvania to live with her grandmother on the family farm. TJ picks back up where she left off eight years earlier, tending to the fruit and nut tree orchard, while learning her grandmother's secret trade. Soon, TJ's high school sweetheart and the same girl who broke her heart, comes back into her life, threatening to steal it away once again. As the weeks turn into months and tragedy strikes again, TJ realizes coming home was the best thing she could've ever done.

Special Assignment by Austen Thorne. Secret Service Agent Parker Meeks has her hands full when she gets her new assignment, protecting a Congressman's teenage daughter, who has had threats made on her life and been whisked away to a Christian boarding school under an alias to finish out her senior year. Parker is fine with the assignment, until she finds out she has to go undercover as a Canon Priest. The last thing Parker expects to find is a beautiful, art history teacher, who is intrigued by her in more ways than one.

Miracle at Christmas by Sydney Canyon. A Modern Twist on the Classic Scrooge Story. Dylan is a power-hungry lawyer who pushed away everything good in her life to become the best defense attorney in the, often winning the worst cases and keeping anyone with enough money out of jail. She's visited on Christmas Eve by her deceased law partner, who threatens her with a life in hell like his own, if she doesn't change her path. During the course of the night, she is taken on a journey through her past, present, and future with three very different spirits.

Bella Vita by Sydney Canyon. Brady is the First Officer of the crew on the *Bella Vita*, a luxury charter yacht in the Caribbean. She enjoys the laidback island lifestyle, and is accustomed to high profile guests, but when a U.S. Senator charters the yacht as a gift to his beautiful twin daughters who have just graduated from college and a few of their friends, she literally has her hands full.

Brides *(Bridal Series book 2)* by Graysen Morgen. Britton Prescott is dating the love of her life, Daphne Attwood, after a few tumultuous events that happened to unravel at her sister's wedding reception, seven months earlier. She's happy with the way things are, but immense pressure from her family and friends to take the next step, nearly sends her back to the single life. The idea of a long engagement and simple wedding are thrown out the window, as both families take over, rushing Britton and Daphne to the altar in a matter of weeks.

Cypress Lake by Graysen Morgen. The small town of Cypress Lake is rocked when one murder after another happens. Dani Ricketts, the Chief Deputy for the Cypress Lake Sheriff's Office, realizes the murders are linked. She's surprised when the girl that broke her heart in high school has not only returned home, but she's also Dani's only suspect. Kristen Malone has come back to Cypress Lake to put the past behind her so that she can move on with her life. Seeing Dani Ricketts again throws her off-guard, nearly derailing her plans to finally rid herself and her family of Cypress Lake.

Crashing Waves by Graysen Morgen. After a tragic accident, Pro Surfer, Rory Eden, spends her days hiding in the surf and snowboard manufacturing company that she built from the ground up, while living her life as a shell of the person that she once was. Rory's world is turned upside when a young surfer pursues her, asking for the one thing she can't do. Adler Troy and Dr. Cason Macauley from Graysen Morgen's best seller, *Falling Snow,* make an appearance in this romantic adventure about life, love, and letting go.

Bridesmaid of Honor *(Bridal Series book 1)* by Graysen Morgen. Britton Prescott's best friend is getting married and she's the maid of honor. As if that isn't enough to deal with, Britton's sister announces she's getting married in the same month and her maid of honor is her best friend

Daphne, the same woman who has tormented Britton for years. Britton has to suck it up and play nice, instead of scratching her eyes out, because she and Daphne are in both weddings. Everyone is counting on them to behave like adults.

Falling Snow by Graysen Morgen. Dr. Cason Macauley, a high-speed trauma surgeon from Denver meets Adler Troy, a professional snowboarder and sparks fly. The last thing Cason wants is a relationship and Adler doesn't realize what's right in front of her until it's gone, but will it be too late?

Fate vs. Destiny by Graysen Morgen. Logan Greer devotes her life to investigating plane crashes for the National Transportation Safety Board. Brooke McCabe is an investigator with the Federal Aviation Association who literally flies by the seat of her pants. When Logan gets tangled in head games with both women will she choose fate or destiny?

Just Me by Graysen Morgen. Wild child Ian Wiley has to grow up and take the reins of the hundred year old family business when tragedy strikes. Cassidy Harland is a little surprised that she came within an inch of picking up a gorgeous stranger in a bar and is shocked to find out that stranger is the new head of her company.

Love Loss Revenge by Graysen Morgen. Rian Casey is an FBI Agent working the biggest case of her career and madly in love with her girlfriend. Her world is turned upside when tragedy strikes. Heartbroken, she tries to rebuild her life. When she discovers the truth behind what really happened that awful night she decides justice isn't good enough, and vows revenge on everyone involved.

Natural Instinct by Graysen Morgen. Chandler Scott is a Marine Biologist who keeps her private life private. Corey Joslen is intrigued by Chandler from the moment she meets her. Chandler is forced to finally open her life up to Corey. It backfires in Corey's face and sends her running. Will either woman learn to trust her natural instinct?

Secluded Heart by Graysen Morgen. Chase Leery is an overworked cardiac surgeon with a group of best friends that have an opinion and a reason for everything. When she meets a new artist named Remy Sheridan at her best friend's art gallery she is captivated by the reclusive woman. When Chase finds out why Remy is so sheltered will she put her career on the line to help her or is it too difficult to love someone with a secluded heart?

In Love, at War by Graysen Morgen. Charley Hayes is in the Army Air Force and stationed at Ford Island in Pearl Harbor. She is the commanding officer of her own female-only service squadron and doing the one thing she loves most, repairing airplanes. Life is good for Charley, until the day she finds herself falling in love while fighting for her life as her country is thrown haphazardly into World War II. Can she survive being in love and at war?

Fast Pitch by Graysen Morgen. Graham Cahill is a senior in college and the catcher and captain of the softball team. Despite being an all-star pitcher, Bailey Michaels is young and arrogant. Graham and Bailey are forced to get to know each other off the field in order to learn to work together on the field. Will the extra time pay off or will it drive a nail through the team?

Submerged by Graysen Morgen. Assistant District Attorney Layne Carmichael had no idea that the sexy woman she took home from a local bar for a one night stand would turn out to be someone she would be prosecuting months later. Scooter is a Naval Officer on a submarine who changes women like she changes uniforms. When she is accused of a heinous crime she is shocked to see her latest conquest sitting across from her as the prosecuting attorney.

Vow of Solitude by Austen Thorne. Detective Jordan Denali is in a fight for her life against the ghosts from her past and a Serial Killer taunting her with his every move. She lives a life of solitude and plans to keep it that way. When Callie Marceau, a curious Medical Examiner, decides she wants in on the biggest case of her career, as well as, Jordan's life, Jordan is powerless to stop her.

Igniting Temptation by Sydney Canyon. Mackenzie Trotter is the Head of Pediatrics at the local hospital. Her life takes a rather unexpected turn when she meets a flirtatious, beautiful fire fighter. Both women soon discover it doesn't take much to ignite temptation.

One Night by Sydney Canyon. While on a business trip, Caylen Jarrett spends an amazing night with a beautiful stripper. Months later, she is shocked and confused when that same woman re-enters her life. The fact that this stranger could destroy her career doesn't bother her. C.J. is more terrified of the feelings this woman stirs in her. Could she have fallen in love in one night and not even known it?

Fine by Sydney Canyon. Collin Anderson hides behind a façade, pretending everything is fine. Her workaholic wife and best friend are both oblivious as she goes on an emotional journey, battling a potentially hereditary disease that her mother has been diagnosed with. The only person who knows what is really going on, is Collin's doctor. The same doctor, who is an acquaintance that she's always been attracted to, and who has a partner of her own.

Shadow's Eyes by Sydney Canyon. Tyler McCain is the owner of a large ranch that breeds and sells different types of horses. She isn't exactly thrilled when a Hollywood movie producer shows up wanting to film his latest movie on her property. Reegan Delsol is an up and coming actress who has everything going for her when she lands the lead role in a new film, but there one small problem that could blow the entire picture.

Light Reading: A Collection of Novellas by Sydney Canyon. Four of Sydney Canyon's novellas together in one book, including the bestsellers *Shadow's Eyes* and *One Night*.

Visit us at www.tri-pub.com